NADINE LITTLE

We Are Not Conquered

The Warrior Angels 3

LITTLE PUBLISHING

Cover design by 100 Covers.

This book is written in British English.

First edition

ISBN: 978-1-915999-02-3

This book was professionally typeset on Reedsy.
Find out more at reedsy.com

Sign up to my mailing list to get a free bonus epilogue. Members of my mailing list get other free stuff and exclusive behind-the-scenes material.

Members are always the first to hear about my new books and discounts.

See the back of the book for details on how to join.

'It is not enough to conquer;
one must learn to seduce.'
Voltaire

'"One last fight, my love.
Together, this time,"
she whispered.'
Emily A. Duncan

1

The woman on the table looks like a goddess—white, shining hair, cheekbones sharp enough to slice anyone who dares to touch, curves that should be illegal encased in a black leather bodice and a skirt split to the thigh.

Except she's not a woman.

Gold-rimed wings drape to the floor, the feathers as perfect and pale as her smooth skin. Plump lips pout in repose, like any sleeping princess awaiting true love's first kiss.

But she's no angel, either. I still remember her promise to violate me with her knife.

I shiver against the strong arms holding me. "I'm not sure I should be here."

Abayankari was one of thousands of alien-made creations to come to Earth on a hostile mission. My relationship with one of their kind sparked an uprising that saved us all.

"She will not hurt you," Hunter growls in my ear, his warmth a familiar comfort at my back. "She will regret it if she tries."

"She will not try," Uziyah scoffs from his position beside the table, his gaze on Abayankari. "She will have other things to capture her attention."

"I'm sorry it's taken so long," I say softly.

His silver eyes flick to me. "Someone had to be the last."

1

Uziyah has always had a soft spot for Abayankari, even when she was psychotic. Aboard the Protectorate spaceship that was meant to be my final resting place and Hunter's prison, their dominance fights were legendary.

Until Uziyah switched to my side.

He bows his head to the unconscious warrior. A waterfall of sunflower-yellow hair slides forward to hide his face. Golden wings curl to cover his bared torso and the loose, linen trousers he favours. Quite a contrast to Hunter and his love of black.

Eight months have passed since we captured the spaceship and returned home. Eight months of treating the Protectorate to destroy the cybernetics in their brains. All seven thousand and fifty-two of them. I worried keeping them sedated for so long would have lasting consequences, but I should know not to doubt the constitution of warrior angels. Except when it comes to iron. We had to keep switching the type of anaesthetic gas every few days since their bodies adapted to it. Thankfully, the Protectorate ship had plenty to choose from, otherwise we would've had a huge problem when they started waking up as violent and cruel as they were programmed to be. We built, borrowed, and stole more MRI machines for the underground facility near Roslin, just outside Edinburgh. The place has become my second home.

On the table, Abayankari stirs. White lashes flutter on flawless cheeks. Beautiful turquoise eyes open and fix on me.

The colour is the same as the floor of the Protectorate ship, which is now a monument on Arthur's Seat, the dormant volcano that hulks over Edinburgh like a slumbering elephant. It was the last place she saw me, almost two years ago now. For her, it'll feel like she just shut her eyes for a minute.

It's taken me months to recover from that nightmare.

2

Another shiver vaults down my spine. Hunter squeezes me in reassurance, the silk of his wings brushing my bare arms. I want to be outside, enjoying the heat of an unseasonably warm September, not down here in the perpetual coolness that reminds me of the angels' spaceship.

A frown wrinkles Abayankari's brow. She sits up. Only Hunter's body prevents me from retreating.

"You stabbed me," she says slowly.

Her fingers find the rents in her bodice over her ribs and gut, the flesh beneath long healed. She examines her fingertips, as if expecting sickly froth and blood.

"Yet I feel no desire to rip your limbs from your sockets." She tilts her head. "Why is that?"

"You've been asleep for a while, 'Kari," Uziyah says. "Much has changed."

Her gaze zips to him. She narrows her eyes.

"Uziyah," she snarls.

She leaps from the table. She may be slim, but she's tall and muscled. She slams Uziyah's bulk into the wall, her legs clamped to his ribs. The flapping of wings fills the air. Hunter's arms tighten, stopping me from intervening, as if I could separate them like two squalling cats.

"She's hurting him," I gasp.

"They are not fighting, Maia."

"But—"

"*Look.*"

Uziyah breaks Abayankari's hold and tosses her across the room. She sails over the table and bounces off the one-way glass, no doubt scaring the crap out of the watching facility personnel. Uziyah vaults the table and greets her, his agility always a surprise considering the size of him. He spins

Abayankari and bends her over the table. She purrs, grinding her arse into his crotch.

Oh. Okay. *Not* fighting.

A blush heats my cheeks.

"Uh, maybe we should leave and let these two catch up," I say.

Hunter's chuckle rumbles in my ear. "Perhaps we should. And perhaps I would like to do my own 'catching up.'"

The heat travels from my cheeks to my belly. Hunter's fingers flex on my hips, his arms crossed beneath my breasts.

Abayankari slaps her wings shut, sandwiching Uziyah between them. She thrusts backwards, and he stumbles. Before he can regain his footing, she wraps herself around him, wings and limbs and all, and sinks her teeth into his throat. An expression of rapture fills Uziyah's face. He sags into the one-way glass. The hand I can see disappears into the slit of Abayankari's skirt and palms her rump. She claws at his chest, raising pale streaks of abused flesh. He groans, but not in pain.

"As long as our catching up isn't as rough as theirs," I whisper as Hunter backs away from the mauling couple, carrying me with him.

"Maia," he says in his low and husky voice, "for you, I will always be gentle. But I will still make you scream."

The door opens on silent hinges. My last glimpse of the room shows Abayankari's skirt bunched around her waist and her hands ripping Uziyah's trousers open. Neither of them is wearing underwear.

My poor eyeballs.

The WACO soldier—though we may need to change the name since the warrior angels are no longer the ones we need to counter—stares at us with wide eyes.

Her fingers blanch on her rifle. "Should I—should I call for backup?"

Hunter gives her his implacable face and says, "They are sexing," then he turns on his heel and strides down the corridor before she can do more than gape. My feet don't touch the floor.

I stifle a giggle. "Maybe we should've warned Uziyah and Abayankari that they're being watched."

"They are used to being watched. They revel in it."

"Oh. Uh, do you…?"

His lips nibble my ear.

"I do not like witnesses. I am the only one who gets to see you come undone," he purrs.

And with that, he whisks me back to our flat in Martello Court to be thoroughly and expertly unravelled.

2

"They are becoming restless."

Lieutenant General Thomas Curran hustles down the nondescript corridor of the research facility, the rest of us scrabbling to keep up in his wake. And by the rest of us, I mean me and Greg. Hunter and Devinon match the pace easily, Dev pushing Steph in her wheelchair, one of his sapphire wings brushing the wall. Steph reclines like the queen she is, her bedazzled cane tucked into its holster on the side of the arm rest. Her chestnut wig complements her plum-coloured skirt and heels.

The Lieutenant General reminds me of those Easter Island statues—every part of him solid and blocky, though his khaki uniform fits him perfectly. He glances over his shoulder, the metal emblem on his cap catching the light.

"They're in the containment room," he says. "It was modelled after an area of their ship, so I assumed the familiarity would be comforting."

My footsteps stutter. A warm hand steadies my back. Greg slides me an understanding look from my other side.

Nothing on that ship held an ounce of comfort.

"But they've all been through your orientation, right?" I say, hurrying to regain my momentum. "Abayankari was the last, and she awoke yesterday."

6

"They have all been briefed on the situation," Curran says, not turning this time. "That is when they got restless."

And that's when they called me. Because as well as being the leader of two rebellions, I'm also now the soother of restless angels.

"What was their opinion on the situation?"

My question earns me a glance from the marching military man.

"I did not ask," he says.

Well, okay then.

As far as I can gather from my limited knowledge of all things army, the Lieutenant General is high up in the ranks, responsible for preparing forces for battle. But I guess he's used to commanding, not asking.

Like a certain pair of Creators I know. Or knew? Maybe their carcasses are still trussed in the escape pod, floating forever in the Oort Cloud with the rest of the space junk.

I suppress a shudder and follow Curran's square shoulders until the corridor widens into an antechamber. Ten WACO soldiers stand guard, clutching their iron-filled rifles in front of a huge pair of metal doors. At a nod from Curran, two men heave each half of the entrance open. Another wall of black-clad soldiers greets us. Their commander strides through and I shadow him, everyone else slotting into single file behind me. The press of bodies blocks my view, but I keep my head down, concentrating on not clipping Curran's heels. The space feels large and eerily silent.

Four steps lead upwards onto a narrow stage. Dev hoists Steph and her wheelchair into his arms, his face serene. No clench of effort. I lift my eyes and stare out at the exposed vastness of the room. My gasp echoes. The glittering eyes of thousands of warrior angels focus on me.

"Why would you model it on *that?*" I say, the words strangled.

Smooth walls form a rough oval above a shimmering gold floor. Instead of spectator boxes with purple ferns and elaborate railings, several levels have observation booths protected by strengthened glass, scientists in lab coats silhouetted against harsh light as they peer down at us.

My chest squeezes, forcing my heartbeat into my throat. Gentle fingers clasp mine. Velvet feathers curl around my shoulders in a welcome blanket of heat.

I'm not in space or on that awful ship. It's just a large room buried underground. There are other differences, too. The roof is solid and bare without a transparent rectangle onto the coldness of stars. The floating bed pallets have been commandeered from the Protectorate vessel, making the area a disconcerting amalgamation of the arena and the sleeping quarters. Haughty angels stare down at me, the flicker of a wing the only movement. Uziyah gives me a serious nod from his perch above the stage. Abayankari spoons him from behind, her shining white hair spilling over his shoulders to mix with sunflower yellow. The pallets are the same as they always were—narrow and thin, minus the luxury of a cushion.

I frown and turn to Curran. "You didn't think to give them extra padding for their beds?"

"This is what they're used to, is it not?" he says, matching my frown.

"We're not here to just give them what they're used to. We're not Creators."

I sweep my gaze over the gathered warriors. All their feathers are white and gold, the favoured form of the Protectorate.

Barring Hunter, and Dev at my back with his sapphire wings,

our Jewels—angels with gem-coloured wings—are off on other tasks. They remained behind after the apocalypse, before we were all kidnapped by the Creators, and remembered how to mingle with humans when their cybernetics were removed. So they have the freedom and trust to travel as they please.

We're not quite there with the white and golden varieties, even though none of them have been violent since we removed the crap from their brains. They're still intense. Trained to kill. Rigidly expressionless. They don't trust *us* yet. And I don't blame them. Our uneasy truce could shatter on the whisper of a wing.

"I can't believe you're still wearing that thing," Steph says on my right, keeping her voice low. Hunter eases back to give her space as she nudges her wheelchair to the edge of the stage.

Curran on my left probably can't hear her, but no doubt every angel in the room can. They have superior hearing, superior eyesight, superior strength.

Superior everything.

I glance at my fingers stroking the strap of the command hub on my wrist. I'm used to the heft of it. The smoothness of the screen under my fingertips.

"You won't step foot on the spaceship, but you're all right with torture bling from the *Jurassic Park* twins."

My lips twitch, which I'm sure was Steph's intention. My best friend has an uncanny ability to know when I'm about to lose my shit.

Who knew you could get claustrophobic in a room as giant as this. Of course, my anxiety isn't helped by the judgement and expectation of thousands of angels.

"Check this out, though," I say, my voice only a little reedy. Maybe no one will notice.

Hunter's feathers tickle across my arms from his new position immediately behind me.

He notices everything.

I tap the device, then tilt my wrist to show Steph. The words 'No cybernetics detected' fill the screen.

"Pretty cool, huh?"

Steph wrinkles her nose. "I'd still smash it."

"I don't want to make the scientists cry."

On our return to Earth, they'd taken the two command hubs belonging to the Creators, Salam and Tallai, for study. They would have kept them if I hadn't requested—then demanded—one back. I'm not sure why I was so adamant, especially with the memories it evokes of where it came from and what it was used for. Who wore it.

I swipe my finger across the screen where the alien symbols of an ancient language have been translated into English.

"You are making them more restless," Curran hisses between his teeth.

I jerk my head up. Feathers rustle. The angels remain stoic, yet a gentle sway runs amongst them, like the wind blowing through grass. I hold my arm aloft, turning the screen of the command hub outwards.

Warrior angels don't flinch, but their attention stabs at the device that was used to hurt them.

"This can't control you anymore," I say. "No one can control you anymore."

Curran shifts next to me. I scan the angels, crowded shoulder to shoulder on the shimmering gold floor and crouched on the floating pallets. The faceless scientists. The weight of the roof and soil above. Everything bathed in too-bright light.

"Is there somewhere else we can go? Somewhere with

10

windows?" I say to Curran, not looking at him.

"The above-ground structures are for facility personnel only. And this is the largest space we have."

"Okay, then let's go outside."

"Outside."

It's an incredulous statement, not a question. I turn and catch Curran's slow blink.

"They've not… Have you kept them in this room the whole time they've been awake?"

Curran clears his throat. "Nowhere else is suitable to hold them."

"We're not supposed to *hold them*," I say a bit sharply, if Curran's deepening scowl is any indication. "They're not prisoners."

"They are a hostile force."

"They *were* a hostile force," I snap. "Have you at least been feeding them?"

Curran transfers his weight from one foot to the other, his slab of a face darkening to dusky pink. "They have received rations from their own ship. The ship that's currently treating our ancient and special volcanic site like a car park."

That's hardly the angels' fault. I'm the one who docked it on Arthur's Seat.

"You haven't given them any of our food, not even as a treat?" I say, my voice rising.

"Jesus, man," Greg mutters behind me, "and I thought the Creators were joyless arseholes."

It's probably my fault for distancing myself. For trusting the military and scientists to assimilate the angels. My therapist encouraged me to visit them, now that they're less homicidal.

Curran's face flushes darker. "Their rations were sufficient for their requirements."

My tastebuds shrivel at the thought of the tart, beige glop the warrior angels drank for sustenance. Sure, it met all bodily needs for far longer than any human food, but it got tedious very quickly.

I spin on my heel and stride for the steps.

"Where are you going, Miss Buckthorn?" says the incredulous military man.

I pause on the top stair. Hunter, Greg, Steph, and Dev, only a pace behind me, separate to reveal Curran on the stage.

I wiggle my ring finger at him, the stones and symbols on my wedding band glinting under the lights. "It's Mrs Buckthorn. Hunter took my surname since he doesn't have one of his own. And we're going outside. I think we could all do with some fresh air and sunlight."

"But... but the..." Curran eyes the silent, watchful angels, then hustles closer to me. He leans in and lowers his voice. "If you let them out, there's nothing to stop them from flying away."

"That's right," I say, and he flinches at my normal tone.

His mouth works. I give him ten seconds, but no words spill out. My boots clatter on the steps. The WACO soldiers fidget and cuddle their rifles. Four block the entrance.

"Open the door," I say, hoping my thudding heartbeat can't be heard in my voice.

What the hell will I do if they refuse? It could be a massacre. For them. Their bullets would cut down some of the warriors, but they'd soon be overwhelmed. It's a testament to the absence of the cybernetics that the angels haven't tried to escape already.

After a hesitation that does nothing for my blood pressure, two soldiers stand aside and the remaining two heave the entrance open. I move as soon as the gap is wide enough. The whisper of feathers quickens my pace until I'm almost jogging down the corridor. I barely feel the concrete steps under my feet. Two sets of steel-reinforced doors buzz open. Then it's sunshine and mown grass and a warm breeze with a hint of the chill to come. The leaves on the trees surrounding the facility have started to turn orange and red. I stop at the edge and look back across the field, slightly breathless.

The Protectorate stream from the Roslin Institute. Over seven thousand humans would form a noisy, uncoordinated rabble. But seven thousand warriors move in perfect synchrony, some flying, some walking, but all in regimented lines that would make Curran envious, if I could see him through the approaching ranks.

"Christ, that's terrifying," Greg says off to my left, sandwiched between Steph and Dev. "Even when they're on our side. They are on our side, right?"

"We'll soon find out," I say.

"Not comforting," Greg mutters.

Dev lays a hand on the smaller man's shoulder. "Do not worry, my prickly pear. I will protect you."

Greg huffs, but inches closer to the angel. Steph spares her men a grin before returning her attention to the advancing warriors without a sign of fear on her face. Hunter's steady presence bolsters my right side. I grip his hand for a second, the hard band of his wedding ring biting into my fingers.

The Protectorate halt as one, and silence falls over the field. My heart knocks against my ribs, loud in the quiet. A distant engine swells and fades. A magpie cackles from the trees. Uziyah smirks at me from the front row, his shoulder pressed to Abayankari's. Her turquoise gaze sweeps me from head to toe, and I decide to ignore her considering look instead of fretting about what it means. The warrior angels block my view of the facility, though I can only see the first few rows since I'm significantly shorter than them.

Story of my life.

My voice cracks on my first attempt to speak. Uziyah's smirk morphs into a grin. Glaring at him soothes my nerves, despite my flushed cheeks.

"I'm not sure what Lieutenant General Curran told you," I say, projecting as loudly as I can, "but you have a choice."

Strong hands wrap around my waist and lift me up. I swallow a squeak. Hunter sets me on his broad shoulder, my boots pressed to his chest and his arm across my thighs to steady me. The lofty position offers me a view over the sea of warrior angels. Sunlight gilds golden feathers.

"We are not your creators," I say into the hush. "We won't force you into a life you haven't chosen. On this planet, you have free will. You're not weapons to be used on command."

I drop my gaze to the grass, needing a break from the intense focus of angels. My throat hurts already. I clear it, and raise my eyes again.

"But we do need to ask for your help. *I* need to ask for your help." I pet Hunter's black hair, running the silky strands through my fingers. A wing arches to offer me a backrest. "I don't think we've seen the last of Salam and Tallai."

A shiver of sound passes through the listening angels.

"They'll return to claim their property as they have before," I say when the warriors settle, "and humanity will face their retribution. But this is where you have a choice. You can ally with us—fight with us—and stop the Creators. Or you can choose not to."

14

The echo of my voice fades across the open space. Thousands of angels breathe in and out.

"What if we choose not to fight?" The words drift from the centre of the pack, the speaker unknown.

I shrug, nearly toppling off Hunter's shoulder. "We'll fight them anyway, no matter how many of you choose to stand with us. This is our home. I want it to be your home, too, whether you help us or not."

Somewhere beyond or amongst the press of angels, Curran is no doubt seething in his uniform. He would have ordered the Protectorate to fight, choice be damned.

And I get it. Without the aid of the warrior angels, our likelihood of fending off Salam and Tallai is slim. They have an entire province—ten factions of non-angel creations—to choose from. Who knows what ship they'll send this time. But I won't force anyone to fight. I won't hurt anyone just to get what I want.

A gentle touch achieves more than cruelty and subjugation.

"And what if you lose?" another voice asks.

A grim smile tugs at my mouth. "They'll wipe humanity from the face of this planet and return you all to that ship of nightmares. You'll go back to being cybernetically controlled killing machines. But if we win…"

I meet the eyes of as many warriors as I can.

"If we win, you can stay here and live in peace, however you want."

"What is to stop us from taking the ship and leaving you to your fate?" Abayankari says, one hand on her hip. She's replaced her torn leather for a robe of white belted at the waist.

"Absolutely nothing," I say.

Another ripple of movement stirs the gathered angels,

though their attention doesn't waver from me. A faint squawk towards the facility buildings shows Curran is still with us.

The warriors don't know how to pilot the ship, but I'm sure they'd figure it out. Or I'll show them, if that's their choice.

"The Romshalla Province is but one of countless that polices the universes," Uziyah says. "What if others come to their aid?"

Panic threatens to overwhelm my voice, but I swallow it back.

"Then we hope they listen better than Salam and Tallai. Or we fight them, too."

Uziyah steps forward with a savage grin. "We will fight for you, feeble creature. On one condition."

Hunter's growl vibrates through me from my perch on his shoulder. I squeeze his arm across my thighs.

I kind of like Uziyah's pet name for me. I worked hard for it to be a term of endearment rather than a slur.

"What's your condition?" I say.

Uziyah tilts his head. "We will take orders from no other human. We will heed only you."

"Oh, this is just classic," Steph chuckles, but I can't look at her.

All my focus is on the semi-invincible warrior angel who drops to one knee in front of me.

And, after a single, stuttered heartbeat, the seven thousand others who copy him.

3

My ringtone trills through the dark and cosy room. I try to hold on to sleep, but it slips from my fingers like shadows. Tiredness grits my eyes and sticks them shut. It feels like I only closed them for a second.

When we got home after the angels swore allegiance to me—once Curran had finished his posturing and huffing and dictating—Hunter decided he wanted to do his own kneeling. Except his type of kneeling involved my legs over his shoulders and me screaming his name to the ceiling. The rest of the evening disappeared with me in his lap, then bent over the couch, then on the living room rug.

My warrior angel has magnificent stamina. He had to carry my boneless body to bed since I'm just a fragile human.

A fragile human who's suddenly in charge of an army. How the bloody hell did that happen? A selfish part of me was hoping I wouldn't be needed. That the Global Protection Alliance and WACO teams could take it from here. After everything we suffered on the Protectorate ship, I just want to spend my days in some semblance of normality with Hunter and my friends.

Until Salam and Tallai arrive to ruin it, of course. *If* they arrive. Maybe they'll heed the warning I gave when I left them in the escape pod. Maybe the Protectorate will finally leave us alone. We're a tiny blue marble in the infinity of space; why start an interstellar war for one rogue ship?

Probably because they'll crush us as easily as stomping on an ant colony. And Salam is too much of an arsehole to let disobedience slide.

"Maia," Hunter whispers.

A gentle hand shakes my bare shoulder. He arches above me, a creature of blackness. The phone peals merrily in his other hand, the light of the screen caressing his cheekbones and turning his eyes into pools of night.

"I'm awake," I grumble.

I reluctantly relinquish my pocket of warmth under the duvet and sit up, the covers dropping to my waist. Delicate flesh puckers in the cooler air, and Hunter's appreciative purr chases goosebumps across my skin. My flapping hand finds the lamp switch, bathing the room in yellow light. Not that Hunter needs it to ogle my boobs with his night-penetrating eyeballs. He smirks and passes me the noisy phone. One hand curls around my hip and drags me into the cage of his body, pressing our nakedness together and surrounding me with his addictive scent of ice.

I glance at the phone screen and accept the call, silencing the insistent jingle. "Bronwyn, do you know what time it is?"

"Why, yes, child. It is precisely eight minutes past two in the morning, your time."

The buzzes and clicks of the Creators' language underlie the English words, translated instantly by the nanotech she squirted in my ears when I was a prisoner of Salam and Tallai's hospitality. Bronwyn can speak perfect English, but she prefers her own tongue when she can talk with people who understand it.

I rub my forehead. "I wasn't actually asking for the time."

"Then I do not understand."

"Why are you calling, Bronwyn?" I sigh.

She's been on Earth for almost a year now, but still hasn't grasped all the nuances of our language, though her help was invaluable in creating the translation programme for the command hubs. I picture her in the healing ward of the Protectorate ship, hunched on a metal stool, her scaled wings patterned with diamonds of pale blue and pink, her beak brushed by the light of her phone screen. She still prefers to wear a bodysuit, but unlike the dull mauve she had under Salam and Tallai's command, she has ones made special in fluorescent colours that sear the retinas. She continues to paint her toenails to match.

I miss her. Steph sees her regularly for healing shroud treatments to manage the pain and slow the progression of her fibromyalgia and rheumatoid arthritis. Bronwyn is kept busy by sharing the Creators' medical equipment and has become an actual healer instead of just patching up broken angels to send them out to be mauled again. She's working with the scientists to replicate the technology for widespread use.

"Brace yourself, child," Bronwyn says softly.

I jerk from my relaxed sprawl in Hunter's embrace. His arms tighten. The phone hurts my ear, as if mashing it closer will make the bad news bearable.

"Tell me," I wheeze.

"I received a ship-to-ship communication."

My heart seizes, then flutters in a panic. "What does that mean—a voice message, a video?"

"A text communication."

I force myself to say, "From who?" since the words try to

lodge in my throat.

"From Salam'ack—" She clicks her beak. "From Salam."

Dread swoops in my stomach. I still see his violent, violet eyes in my nightmares. Hear the fractured cackle of his laugh.

"What does it say?"

Bronwyn's wings rustle on the other end of the phone, her scales sliding together as she moves. "I will forward it to you. Do you have the command hub close by?"

I snatch the device from the bedside cabinet and wedge it between my duvet-covered knees. The screen shows nothing but the home menu when I tap it awake.

"How close are they if they can send a text communication? We haven't had any warning."

The GPA assured the world that they'd improved the early-warning network. That we should know if any ships enter our solar system well in advance rather than right when they land on our freaking doorstep and kidnap us into space.

Like last time.

"Ships can communicate across universes, child," Bronwyn says.

My muscles unwind a tiny bit at her soothing tone, though sweat slicks my skin and my heart rate may need an hour or two to calm down.

Hunter nuzzles my temple. "No matter what it says, we will deal with it together. I will not let them touch you again, Maia."

I nod against his lips.

"The communication should be coming through now."

"Thanks, Bronwyn," I say.

"I wish you would visit me, child."

I clear my throat. "I know. Sorry. I'll meet you anywhere but on that ship."

20

The command hub beeps. I swipe the new message icon.

"I am sorry, too, child," Bronwyn says even softer, and hangs up.

The phone slips from my numb fingers anyway. A growl rumbles in Hunter's chest where he's pressed to my back.

On the screen of the command hub, in screaming block capital letters, are the words 'WE ARE COMING FOR YOU.'

4

The staff of the Roslin Institute are surprisingly chipper for three in the morning. They're just doing their normal shift of monitoring the screens and systems in the command centre. They weren't awoken by a phone call and a text message from douchebags who should really stay in their universe and leave ours the fuck alone. The scent of coffee fills the bustling space. A pot of chamomile tea steams on the desk in front of me. The console operator, Yannis, takes a sip from a ceramic mug depicting the solar system. He leans back in his chair and smooths a finger along his neat moustache.

"Are you sure I cannot offer you a seat?" he says, his dark-brown eyes flicking over my shoulder. "Both of you."

Hunter looms behind me, his face a mask of perfect arrogance. He is still and steady while I shift from foot to foot. The hub on my wrist weighs heavier than usual. Dragging me down.

Our appearance caused a stir of excited chatter in the above-ground facility used for watching the stars and communicating with similar complexes across the world. Yannis, as the most senior personnel on shift, got the enviable task of helping us, though there's a suspicious number of people bunched near the other desks in our vicinity, standing and shuffling papers and side-eyeing us with greedy intensity. The entire room is bordered by windows looking out onto the darkness broken only by security lights.

"We're fine, thanks," I say, failing to stifle a yawn. "Has anyone responded to your message yet?"

Yannis turns his attention to the multiple screens filling his concave desk console. A finger continues to stroke his moustache. Endless data scrolls across several monitors. Others show graphs, grainy pictures, and flowing numbers. Telephones ring in the background, the answered conversations a constant, low-level hum.

"Not yet, but as I said when you arrived, we haven't detected any unusual activity on our instruments here." Yannis takes another silent, precise sip of tea. "Are you positive I cannot interest you in a cup of something while you wait? A bottle of water? I'm sure I can round up some cola, if you're so inclined."

"We're good. I'm jittery enough as it is."

"Ha, of course." Yannis clears his throat. "May I see the text again?"

I tap the screen and tilt my wrist, not looking at the words. I've seen them enough. Yannis coughs delicately, then places his mug on his desk.

"Nice of them to warn us."

"Oh, it's not nicety. The Creators want us to stew in the anticipation of our own suffering. They thrive on it."

Hunter eases closer, his presence a warm line at my back. His wings stir the air and tickle my hair across my cheeks. I lean into him, and his hands rest on my hips. His fingers slip under my hoodie to touch skin, replacing the goosebumps of unsettled fear with something more pleasant. I tug my sleeve over the command hub. Yannis jerks his gaze from Hunter's slim, strong fingers at my waist.

"We assumed they would come again." He nods at a white-board on the other side of the room. "We have a bet going."

"What are you betting on?"

"The date their ship will arrive in our orbit." Yannis pours a long stream of yellowish tea into his mug. Steam wisps from the surface. "Your message bodes well for me. My date is the closest."

"How long?"

"Since we have had no sign of their presence in our solar system, and we know it takes twelve months from their worm-hole to Earth thanks to your journey in their commandeered ship, I anticipate they will get here in thirteen months." A quick, nervous smile flashes under Yannis's perfect moustache. "Lucky thirteen."

Thirteen months. That's still... a decent amount of time away. A year of intensive training should easily integrate our human army with the warrior angels and have them working as a unit.

It's fine. Everything will be fine, ominous text be damned.

I glance at the clock in the bottom-right corner of one of Yannis's many monitors. Sixteen minutes past three. Only two hours and forty-four minutes until my meeting with Curran. A meeting I called to placate his blustering and that he scheduled for six in the morning just to be a dick.

Guess I'm not getting anymore sleep tonight.

I sag in Hunter's grip. His arms wrap around my middle and tuck me tight against his torso, his chin on my head. Longing creeps across Yannis's face before he buries it in his mug of chamomile. A jaunty tune blares from the speaker of Yannis's central screen.

"Ah, here we go."

4

He sets his cup on the desk and clicks on the notification box. The bustling behind us falls still. A woman's face appears on the monitor—red-framed glasses, brown hair in a ponytail, the collar of a white shirt tucked over a lilac wool jumper.

"Good evening, Doctor Muldoon," she says, her mouth quirked, "though I suppose it's morning for you thar."

The accent is strong, almost southern. Undoubtedly American. Yannis emailed his contact in NASA headquarters, which is based in Washington DC.

"Doctor Alisand, thank you for calling back so quickly. It may be very early morning here, but, as you know, the stars never sleep."

Her laughter is a deep bark of sound. "Indeed, they do not."

Behind Doctor Alisand, tiered rows of computers and equipment disappear out of sight, some empty. It looks like the control centres you see in movies when they're launching rockets to save the world from a meteor instead of an alien invasion.

Doctor Alisand raises her gaze to meet mine. "I see you have some distinguished guests. We were all quite envious that Scotland got to host the angels ratha than our great, space-farin' nation. Not to mention the religious connotations."

"The next time the Creators want to kidnap someone into another universe, I'll be sure to pass your name along," I say drily.

"The wonders you must have seen, Miss Buckthorn. I can't imagine it."

"Yes, the torture and abuse were all quite wonderful. And it's Mrs."

Shrewd eyes flick upwards to Hunter nestled behind me.

"It's a pleasure to address you, Hunter," she says, though she

25

pronounces it Hunt-a.

"Call me Mr Buckthorn," he says, his voice rumbling against my back.

A shiver quivers through Doctor Alisand's ponytail.

"Fascinating," she breathes.

Yannis shifts in his chair. "If we could return to the matter at hand, Doctor Alisand?"

"Ma apologies. Scientific curiosity got the better of me." She pushes her glasses higher on her nose. "We have reviewed our data in light of this new message. Thar is nothing to indicate the presence of an artificial object from either the Hubble or the James Webb or our radio telescopes. But it may be too soon."

"What does that mean?" I say before Yannis can respond.

"It takes time for light to travel to our instruments, especially from the Oort Cloud. Our readings can only show us the past, not the present."

"What about the shuttle that's been sent out there?"

Representatives from all major space programmes, and research agencies, descended on Arthur's Seat only weeks after I'd parked the Creators' spaceship on the volcano. They retrofitted one of its shuttle vessels with as much equipment as it could hold and blasted it back towards the edge of our solar system.

"The team are still in transit, and asleep," Doctor Alisand says, tucking an escaped tendril of hair behind her ear. "We are getting readings from the automated systems on board, but thar is still a delay."

"But what does that *mean*?"

Her eyes soften despite my frustrated tone.

"It means, Mrs Buckthorn, that our early-warning system

26

will never be as early as we hope."

5

Doctor Alisand's terrifying conclusion keeps the adrenaline flowing and me shakily awake until my meeting with Curran. Hunter flies us to Dreghorn Barracks on the southern edge of Edinburgh beside the City Bypass, the complex surrounded by trees and reminding me of the facility at Roslin. New buildings have been hastily erected where there was once car parks and sports pitches. The barracks were due to be closed before the apocalypse happened, along with Redhorn Barracks, the other army base within Edinburgh's city limits.

Hunter flaps hard and alights in front of a sprawling, single-storey building. Darkness clings to the sky and trees, sunrise at least a half hour away and slowly lightening the horizon to the east. My boots touch the ground, but I stay cradled in Hunter's arms, enjoying the warmth, the chill of our flight settled deep. A flash of sapphire and the rustle of wings announce the arrival of a cheerful Dev carting a grumpy Steph and Greg bundled in jackets, scarfs, and hats.

The unseasonably warm autumn appears to be over, given the thickness of the frost on the ground. Seems almost prophetic.

The Creators could already be in our solar system, powering towards us in a spaceship, and we won't even know it. Last time, the Protectorate appeared without warning and ruined my freaking wedding. Who knows what they'll ruin this time, and how much notice we'll get. A day? A month?

"You okay, Maia?" Steph knocks her shoulder against mine, her pointy bone softened beneath layers. A rainbow scarf covers her mouth and nose, matching the wisps of hair that escape from around the edge of her woollen hat. She looks like a ninja.

If ninjas wear pink, fur-lined coats and skinny jeans.

She had a session with Bronwyn and the healing shroud last night, while I was being thoroughly ravished by Hunter. She won't need her wheelchair or even her cane for a few weeks now.

I show her the message from Salam and fill her in on where we've been at such an ungodly hour. Greg and Dev mutter about the douchebaggery of Creators. Or Greg does. He chooses to stay wrapped in Dev's arms while Steph and I huddle on the flagstones. Hunter spreads his great, black wings to shelter us.

"Fuckers," she hisses. "You know he's doing it to torment you. He could be over a year away, but he wants you cowed and afraid. Have you replied?"

"To his message? Hell no."

"Tell him 'Bring it, you fucking dinosaur.'"

My laugh puffs in a cloud of white. A lick of righteous fury replaces the icy dread in my stomach.

She's right. Why shouldn't I respond? I may be a little mouse compared to the might of his civilisation and the infinity of the universes, but damned if I'll cower for him ever again.

Everyone should have a best friend like Steph. She's my backbone.

I dig my phone from my pocket and dial Bronwyn. She answers with, "Good morning, child. I did not expect to hear from you so soon," instead of complaining about the unsociable hour. She probably hasn't slept since we last spoke, either.

"Morning, Bronwyn. Can you respond to Salam's text message?"

There's a long pause.

"I can," she finally says.

Greg shuffles his feet, the only part of him visible except for his head, the rest of him cocooned in sapphire feathers, like an exotic grub.

"Can't we do this inside?" he grumbles. "I bet it's warmer in there."

Dev squeezes the man in his arms. "My poor prickly pear needs to defrost."

Greg's cheekbones flush, and Steph's grin equals mine. I cover the phone with my hand.

"We're waiting on someone. I asked the rest of the angels to send a representative."

"We could wait inside," Greg huffs. "They're staring at us."

We turn as one to look at the building. The roof is a sharp slope of grey slate tiles to yellow-painted walls and mullioned windows. Faces peer through the glass beside an ornate wooden door bordered by black metal studs and bathed in light from a lantern above. They duck out of sight.

"Hello? Child?" Bronwyn's muffled voice comes from the phone in my hand.

I press the device back to my ear. "Sorry, Bronwyn. Got distracted. I want you to reply to Salam."

I tilt my head and watch the stars fade as the sky brightens towards dawn. I picture the vastness of space separating me

30

from the malevolence of the Creators. Salam's smugness at the thought of my fear.

Well, he's not the only one who can threaten.

"Tell him *we will not be merciful,*" I growl.

Steph directs her grin at me and punches my arm. "Swallow that, you big vulture. I hope he still has the taste of Greg's sock in his gob."

"Do you wish me to add that to the message?" Bronwyn says.

I chuckle. "No, just the merciful bit."

"Then it has been sent."

"Thanks, Bronwyn. I'll talk to you later."

I slide my phone back in my pocket.

I hope Salam and Tallai remember. The escape pod. Trussed in bandages and wire with the tart taste of the food mixture on their tongues. Plus Greg's socks. I told them they'd received the last of my mercy if they ever got free and decided to seek me out.

And this time, I have their army.

Churning wings disturb the pre-dawn hush. Uziyah lands gently for a man of his stature, tucking his gold-rimmed wings against his back. His torso is bare despite the frost, the rest of him clothed in loose trousers with a belt of material knotted at his hip. Abayankari settles next to him, her robe the same colour as her shining hair.

Cool, silver eyes appraise my husband. "Hunter."

Hunter returns the stiff nod and sneer. "Uziyah."

A grin splits Uziyah's face when he switches his attention to me.

"Feeble creature, you will be proud of us," he says, ignoring Hunter's snarl. "I introduced a human custom. We voted."

As if I needed further evidence of the cybernetics cruel

influence. Before, the warriors would have fought each other for the privilege.

My gaze slides to Abayankari. "And you both won the vote to be the representative?"

"I won," Uziyah says, puffing his chest out. "'Kari was a close second."

Abayankari slots herself into his side and strokes her hand across his broad pecs. It awakens an awful memory of her in the arena of the Protectorate ship, clothed in black leather and pawing at Hunter, malice on both their faces. The promise of cruelty and pain.

"Where Uzi' goes, I go," she says.

"Uzi'," Steph snorts.

Abayankari narrows her eyes. "And how do you address your lover?"

"Which one?" I snigger.

Steph's jaggy elbow digs into my side.

"Fair point," she coughs. "Isn't it about time we went inside?"

"Finally," Greg sighs.

Blue bear—that's what she calls Dev. Greg is prickles. I don't have a cutesy name for Hunter. He's just Hunter. My semi-indestructible warrior angel. My soulmate.

I guide my little posse into the building and the door clunks shut behind us. Greg moans at the wash of heat. Two people in front of a low desk watch us with wide eyes. Framed medals and photos of soldiers in uniform decorate the wall behind the desk, maroon chairs lining the other walls. A single glass door leads out of the squat reception area.

"We… we weren't expecting quite so many of you," says a man not much taller than me. His shirt and dress trousers are so starched, they look like they could stand up by themselves.

"I'll take you through, Mrs Buckthorn. The rest of your party can wait here. Do they—do they want something to drink?"

"They're coming with me."

The man's throat bobs. He flicks a glance at his cohort—another man with a crisp shirt and trousers combo—who scuttles around the desk, head bowed, and sinks into the chair.

"The Lieutenant General only invited—"

"I know who he invited. You're making us late."

The door lock clunks, and a buzzer sounds. The first man glares at the guy behind the desk, who doesn't meet his gaze.

"Fine. Follow me, please."

The man yanks the glass door harder than necessary, cutting off the incessant buzz. The corridor beyond is carpeted in maroon, and stretches both ways. We follow the man to the left—three humans padding along and four angels ghosting silently. The room he enters is bare except for a wide table in the centre. Lieutenant General Curran sits with his hands folded on top, flanked by an older man who has pocked scars on his cheek and a woman with auburn hair going grey and kept in a tight bun, all of them in immaculate khaki uniforms and caps. Collar badges shine under the lights. The Pentland Hills are dark humps through the window at their backs. A single empty chair faces them across the expanse of table.

How interrogatory.

I feel somewhat under-dressed in my jacket and hoodie. Hunter is wearing his usual laced black top, trousers, and knee-high boots. Dev favours shirts in varying shades of blue, and jeans, which was never an option under the yoke of the Creators.

He likes how they grip his arse and thighs, according to Steph.

"Mrs Buckthorn," Curran says, his skin blanching under the

clasp of his fingers, "I believe you were the only one invited to this meeting."

"And I believe it benefits everyone to have representatives of all those directly involved." I turn to the reception man hovering on the threshold. "Could we have two more chairs brought in, please? Warrior angels prefer to stand."

He hesitates until Curran grants him a minuscule nod. Two chairs are whisked into the room with military efficiency. Steph unwraps herself from her rainbow hat and scarf and flumps into a seat. Greg unzips his jacket a millimetre. I sit in the middle, flanked by my best friends and mirroring Curran and his subordinates opposite us. Except they don't have angels at their backs. The man from reception tip-toes out and shuts the door.

Curran straightens an already straight shirt sleeve. "The reason I scheduled this meeting, Mrs Buckthorn—"

"Call me Maia."

"—is to ensure we train and deploy the resources we have in the most efficient way possible."

"And we are all for that."

The scrunch of Curran's slab face tells me he wasn't finished.

"With that in mind," he continues, yanking on his other shirt sleeve, "the warrior angels should be assigned to the command of someone within the GPA or, at the very least, the British Army. Such as myself."

"We will follow the fee—Maia," Uziyah says with only a slight hitch. "No one else."

"But if… Maia… were to order you to obey my instructions, would you not follow them?"

"We follow Maia," Uziyah says.

Curran gives me a pointed look. I spread my hands.

34

"The warrior angels are mine. But—"

The officer on Curran's left tuts. "Young lady, this is a matter of global security. You do not have the training or experience to lead such a force. Lieutenant General Curran should be responsible for the Warrior Angel Major Unit—"

"WAMU," Greg chuckles.

"—according to British Army structure. We cannot leave the fate of this planet in the hands of a… girl."

The officer at Curran's right hand narrows her grey eyes at her colleague and opens her mouth, but Steph jerks forward, her pink jacket crinkling.

"Excuse me, arse—"

Greg's hand shoots across my lap under the table and a finger pokes Steph in the ribs.

"—Mr Military Man," Steph says, "but Maia has led two successful rebellions and piloted an enemy spaceship safely to Earth between freaking universes. You wouldn't have the warrior angels on your side if it weren't for her. What have you done except fail to defeat them in the first place and keep us safe from being abducted when they attacked again, Officer…?"

"It's Major General Reynold," the man sniffs, wrinkling his bulbous nose and the grey and drooping moustache beneath. The scars on his cheek deepen at his displeasure.

Curran pats a placating hand on the table. "And while we appreciate her efforts and her sacrifice, we are simply saying that how we proceed is crucial. Do you truly want the responsibility of preparing an army for war?"

"The warrior angels are mine," I say a touch hotly. "Do I want to be responsible for them all? No, but I *earned* it."

Steph and Greg's hands find my thighs and soothe me with a coordinated squeeze under the table. Hunter looms closer, drawing the eyes of the three soldiers opposite us.

"However," I say, dragging their attention back to me, "had the Major General allowed me to finish, I was going to say I can't do it alone. Our armies need to work together to counter the Creators. We work together, we train together, we fight together, and we make them regret ever coming here."

"Yes!" Greg hisses, punching his fist into his palm. *"Nemo me impune lacessit."*

Looks like I've finally managed a rousing speech.

"The warrior angels are already an impeccable and near-indestructible fighting force." Feathers rustle behind me, preening. "They've trained and battled together for goodness knows how long. They're the only ones who can withstand other Protectorate in hand-to-hand combat." Reynold bristles at that, though I plough on. "But we do have one advantage."

Curran tilts his blocky head. "And what is that?"

"Guns," I say.

6

The morning sky darkens with warrior angels. Fear cramps my gut, despite knowing they're on our side. Wings churn the air. Jewel colours break the golden and white monotony, like slashes of paint on a canvas.

"Christ, man, that's no less terrifying," Greg says beside me.

I'm not sure how Uziyah managed to wrangle them so quickly. It's been twenty minutes since our meeting ended and we flew above Curran's army jeep, following him out to a firing range on the slope of Castlelaw Hill, which forms part of the Pentland Hills close to the Roslin Institute. I guess discipline is in their blood. Uziyah would have had to contact the Jewels separately, since they all have their own homes from when they remained behind after the apocalypse, and we welcomed them. After some imprisonment, of course.

"Takes your breath away, doesn't it?" Steph agrees, one arm looped through his, Dev mirroring her on her left. Hunter squeezes my hand, our fingers slotted together.

We crane our necks to watch the descent of the warrior angel army. Curran stands by his jeep parked on the gravel, with his lackey, Reynold, and Brigadier Haile—the woman from the meeting room.

She pulled me aside on my way out, after Curran and I had

hashed through a few details and readjusted our expectations. She apologised for Reynold—not that she should be the one apologising, in my opinion. She said his comments were inappropriate, and she was glad I was on their team. She thought I was an inspiration.

It's always weird to hear. I can barely inspire myself to brush my hair in the morning, never mind stirring it in others.

Uziyah lands in front of me, his chin held high and his expression smug. Abayankari settles next to him as the rest of the angels form their perfect rows on a strip of mown grass about fifty metres wide and surrounded by the spiky green of gorse bushes. The firing range extends at least half a kilometre towards a heather-clad hill, and is broken by lines of coloured targets, quickly swamped by the sheer number of warriors. Red lights on poles flash, spaced regularly from the crest of the hill and disappearing down the slope, marking the boundaries of the firing range for safety and indicating that it's in use. A second, shorter firing range sits off to our left, at least half the size of the one we're standing on.

Curran marches over to me, giving Hunter a wide berth, and holds out a blue and white megaphone. "Time to address your troops," he says to my cocked eyebrow.

Right. Address my troops. I can do that.

Though none of them had trouble hearing me when I spoke at Roslin.

I take the handle, avoiding the button. The megaphone is surprisingly light. I put my mouth to the speaker box and press the trigger. A siren noise blares from the trumpet end. I squeak and drop the megaphone. It bounces off my toe.

"Jesus Christ, my brain," Greg says, a finger in his ear.

Curran scoops the device from the ground and flicks a sliding switch. Reynold smirks at me. Haile crosses her arms and frowns at him. Heat fills my cheeks, but I take the megaphone. I brace myself, and press the trigger.

No horrible wail. Progress.

"Okay, uh... hello. Wow, does my voice really sound like that?" The words echo over the firing range and the silently watching angels. My cheeks flame hotter, and I clear my throat. "Okay. Um, okay."

"Stop saying okay," Steph whispers out the corner of her mouth, eliciting a snort from Greg.

"Right," I say, loud and amplified through the megaphone.

"Much better," Steph says.

I clear my throat again. "Right, so, we all know you're well trained with bows and arrows, and bladed weapons." I pause to share a shiver with Steph and Greg, remembering the awful song of their arrows and the evil blue glow intent on sucking out your soul to leave plant food behind. "But you'll have seen our soldiers use guns that fire iron bullets."

A restless hiss passes through the gathered angels. Very few of them will have been intimately familiar with the iron bullets, even when they abducted me from my wedding. But they'll all have felt the sickly burn of iron and seen the frothy mess it makes when it contacts their blood.

"I brought you here because I want you to be able to use our weapons. I want you to become as deadly with a gun as you were with your bows and arrows. And that training starts today."

While I'm speaking, Reynold sets up a round target on a wooden tripod at the edge of the grass, an embankment of gorse behind it. Circles of white, blue, and yellow surround a tiny, red bullseye.

Curran extends a hand for the megaphone. I pass the device over and he holds out an assault rifle. I blink at it.

"You want me to hold the gun?"

"I want you to shoot the gun, Mrs Buckthorn," he says.

"*Shoot* the gun?" I say slowly. "It's nearly the same size as me!"

I stare at the rifle between us, not letting go of Hunter's hand. The black coating swallows the light and gives nothing back. The long barrel is full of holes I can see through, with a chunky, dimpled thing on the end that I assume is a suppressor.

"A leader should never ask of others what they cannot do themselves," Curran says.

I may or may not imagine the spiteful little glint in his eye. Haile gives me an encouraging nod, but sidles further from the target. Reynold looks like he's enjoying this spectacle immensely.

"What kind of gun is it?" I say out of professional curiosity. Not because I'm stalling.

Shoot a gun—is he mad? I barely managed to hold a sword without cutting myself, though I'm better with one now. Hunter and I still practise twice a week. He gets all hot when I'm proficient with weapons.

I glance at him. His midnight-blue eyes scan the rifle, his face an implacable mask with Curran standing so close.

Hunter would look amazing holding the gun. Intimidating and powerful, especially as it's in his signature colour. I'll look ridiculous. A child playing at soldiers.

"It's a Knight's Stoner rifle, or KS-1," Curran says, though the words mean nothing to me.

"Stoner," Steph chuckles. "Greg, it's made for you."

I don't take my gaze off the weapon, but I imagine there's

some kind of finger or elbow being poked into Steph's ribs. Curran's arm is steady despite holding the gun out for a few minutes now. He's just a solid rectangle of muscle.

Reluctantly, I take the huge hunk of potential death from his grasp. "Wow, it's heavy."

"It's only three kilos," Reynold snorts, earning a scowl from Steph and Haile. He smooths his expression to placid interest.

I hold the gun in my palms, my fingers spread in case I hit something I shouldn't. Text on the right side of the magazine well spells out SR-16 5.66mm Knight's Armament Co. Titusville, Fl USA.

"Would you like me to show you how it works?" Curran says.

I say, "Yes, please," instead of, "*Obviously.*"

He plucks the gun from my hands, and starts pointing at switches and parts. "This is the basic model without the optics, only the iron sights on the barrel. It has an adjustable butt stock and can be used ambidextrously, which is why the same control systems are on both sides. This is the fire selector switch. We'll stick with semi for today. Bolt release. Magazine release. And this is the stance you should take."

He pivots on his heel, sweeps the rifle up and into his shoulder, and squeezes the trigger. There's a loud *pufft*, and a hole appears in the target, nicking the edge of the bullseye.

He slides the triangular butt closer to the body of the weapon, reducing the length of it, then thrusts it at me. "And that's how it's done."

Oh, sure, *that's* how it's done. Easy peasy.

I shuffle to the spot he vacated in front of the target. The rifle sits hard and awkward into the slot of my shoulder. I peer down the two iron sights, one close to my face and the other near the suppressor end. The barrel bobs up and down. My biceps quiver from the weight and the unfamiliar position.

A sound rises, like an approaching wave. Thousands of warrior angels leap into the air and hover in tiered rows, leaving a large cluster on the ground. The wind from their wings stirs my hair and shivers through the spiky gorse bushes.

Ah, good. Now they all have a perfect view of me humiliating myself. Is that Curran's intention? Make me look an idiot so they question their loyalty and decide to follow a competent leader?

I grit my teeth. Screw him. All I need to do is hit the target. I don't care if it's right at the edge. A hit is a win.

"You got this, Maia," Steph says from the sidelines.

I squint down the sights and try to hold the rifle steady. I take a deep breath.

"The safety is still on," Curran says mildly.

I tilt the gun. Sure enough, the little metal pointer sits over the word 'Safe'. I flick it up to 'Semi', careful not to nudge it all the way over to 'Auto'.

"May I adjust your stance, Mrs Buckthorn, without your... husband growling at me?"

I glance at Hunter. His narrowed eyes watch Curran, intense and dark.

"Depends where you touch," I say.

Curran's throat bobs. I get a burst of petty satisfaction at his discomfort. He approaches slowly. Careful hands guide the gun firmly into my shoulder and adjust my grip on the barrel. He sets my index finger along the trigger guard.

"When you're ready, curl your finger around the trigger. The rifle has a two-stage match trigger, meaning the initial pressure you apply prepares the weapon to fire, and only a small increase in pressure after that fires the gun."

Yep. Squeeze and squeeze. Makes sense.

Nerves squirm in my stomach. I aim down the sights. The barrel wavers. I take a deep breath and hold it. The flapping mass of observing angels weighs heavier than the rifle in my hands. On my exhale, I pull the trigger. It shifts easily, then tightens. I keep squeezing. The gun kicks against my shoulder, but I manage not to drop it.

A bullet hole appears perfectly in the centre of the bullseye.

"Holy crap," I whisper.

Steph's whoop nearly has me strafing the bushes. The angels watch, implacable as always, though Uziyah rewards me with a nod. Hunter's breath tickles my nape.

Curran's face is stiff. "Again."

Oh, come on. Can't he let me have my beginner's luck?

I will my heart rate to calm, excited into a canter by my relief at not making a fool of myself in front of all the capable warriors. When it stops trembling through my limbs, I take a couple of steadying breaths, hold it, aim, and fire on the exhale.

At first, I fear I've missed the target entirely. No new holes bloom on the paper. My heart sinks. Curran and Reynold look like they've been forced to eat a bowl of spiders. I stare at the target again.

Oh, my goodness. Is the bullseye...?

"You hit that fucking bullseye twice!" Steph crows. "Of course you're a natural. Of *course* you can pick up a gun and do better than the men who've trained for years. I bet it's all those computer games you play. That first-person shooter shit."

My shaking fingers slide the safety on. I offer the rifle to Curran, hoping my expression is pleasant instead of showing the ecstatic smugness swelling my chest and threatening to burst out in my own cackle of victory.

Take that, you snooty military arsehole.

"Very good, Buckthorn," he says, his stoic statue face in place.

Ooh, Buckthorn. I don't know much about the army, but I do know they call each other by their surnames. Or the lowly soldiers do, anyway. Am I a lowly soldier now? Curran probably wouldn't appreciate it if I returned the favour.

The angels land into their neat rows, wings flapping and settling to silence. Hunter presses close, his solid chest against my back.

"I would like to take you home now," he purrs in my ear.

Heat shoots to my gut. I sag into the warmth of him.

Before I can open my mouth to wholeheartedly agree, Curran says, "Divide your warriors into groups of two hundred. We'll spend the rest of the morning in the classroom on gun mechanics and handling, then do some fitness training in the afternoon."

"Fitness training?" I squeak.

"I hope your stamina is as good as your aim, Buckthorn," he says.

And there's that smug little smile again.

I whip my head around to Steph. She's slightly further away than I remember her being, cuddled under Dev's arm, Greg on Dev's other side.

"You're staying, though, right? You'll do it with me? You and Greg?"

Probably a bit much to expect with her condition, but I can't help the panic in my voice. I can't be the only human non-soldier training with freaking warrior angels.

A glance passes between the trio.

"I'm just the glamorous assistant," Steph says. "I'll hold your gun and cheer from the sidelines. Greg will join, though. But, uh, maybe tomorrow."

"Yeah, man, I'll train with you." Greg clears his throat. "Tomorrow."

The three of them ease back another step as a unit.

"But… where are you going?"

Another glance. Dev scoops them closer into his sides.

"My delicate butterfly and prickly pear wish to sex me," he says with an affectionate smile.

Haile chokes on something behind me. Probably her own saliva.

"You're blowing me off to go have sex?" I say. "In the middle of a global crisis?"

I sound like Reynold. Except for the sex bit.

"Well, we're in the calm before the storm," Steph says, continuing to retreat with her men as we all goggle at her. "Then things will get pretty intense. This is just the start. So… *carpe diem?*"

"Yeah, pluck the day, Maia," Greg says.

"I thought it was seize the day."

"That's a common mistranslation. You still need to read more."

"You cannot abandon your training to go and"—Curran screws up his face—"fornicate. I forbid it."

"You're not my superior." Steph smirks. "Lieutenant General Buckthorn is."

Curran's face collapses further. Reynold appears to be one more gasp away from his head exploding.

"Lieutenant General *Buckthorn!?*" Curran splutters.

I fold my lips to hide a grin. Haile seems to be doing the same.

Steph switches her gaze back to me. "What do you say, Boss?

May I be excused?"

"What the heck," I say, and my grin breaks free. "Go. *Fornicate*. But you better be here tomorrow."

Steph salutes. "Aye aye, LG."

Dev bows his head. "You are a wise and benevolent leader."

"Cheers, Maia!" Greg says.

I laugh as Dev leaps into the air, his sapphire wings blending with the sky. He swoops over the gorse and disappears down the hillside.

I should be mad they're not staying for the very first day of our training. But Curran and Reynold's indignant expressions give me a warm, fuzzy glow.

And some of us should get to have fun.

Before it all goes to hell.

7

Steph

When I finished my last gender reassignment surgery and finally had the body I was meant to have, I never let myself focus too much on relationships. But it was a niggle in my brain—a little voice who worried about whether I'd ever find someone. Someone who'd accept me as I am. I have all the necessary womanly bits, cosmetically if not anatomically, but I'd experienced transphobia from my family—the people who were supposed to love me no matter what. How could I trust a stranger when my own blood cast me out?

That Steph, the early, homeless Steph who possessed only one ill-fitting blonde wig and scuffed cowboy boots, would piss herself with glee if she could see me today. If she knew where she'd end up. BFFs with a woman who's saved the world twice, with some glamorous assistance, and loved by two men who treat her like a queen. Not to mention the wig and shoe collection.

I wish the early Steph had known, through the awkwardness and hatred, all that goodness was coming. Then she never would have felt so alone.

A little twinge of guilt nips me in the ribs for leaving Maia with the military misogynists. For choosing a booty call over learning about guns and crawling in the mud. Hunter will keep her safe, as will the rest of the angels. They watch her with the respect she deserves after we melted the shit in their brains.

I would've fired them all into the Oort Cloud after what they did to her.

She's far more merciful than me. A bleeding-hearted romantic. Just as well. With her warrior angel army, we might actually have a chance against whatever the *Jurassic Park* rejects throw at us.

But in case we don't, I plan to cherish every minute I have left.

"It appears our delicate butterfly is bored with our performance."

The voice tugs my gaze from heeled boots the colour of ripe plums that emphasise my long legs in my skinny jeans. The reclining chair is tucked in the corner opposite the bed, giving me a comfortable view of the two men naked on top of it. A view I was enjoying until my mind wandered and I decided to frown at my feet instead.

"Sorry, blue bear," I say, shifting upright in the chair. "I'm definitely not bored."

Dev kneels on silky sheets only slightly paler than his sapphire wings and eyes. The blinds are drawn against the sun, candlelight flickering across his golden skin and chasing shadows along the curves and dips of muscle. His knees spread Greg's thighs. Greg lies on his back beneath him, his eyes half-lidded and his long, brown hair in disarray on the pillow. Dev pauses the teasing stroke of his velvety feathers. Greg whimpers low in his throat and arches his back, chasing the sensation.

He's so responsive. So *needy*. I never would have guessed it from first knowing him. He was just the guy who lived in my building, smelled of weed, and looked at me askance. I thought he was a transphobe. It took us getting kidnapped by aliens and Dev turned into a monster before the idiot admitted he had feelings for both of us. Now, he's our adorable little geek who loves to be the filling in our couple sandwich.

"Patience, my prickly pear," Dev purrs.

He brushes the tips of his flight feathers over Greg's erection, milking a drop of pre-cum into the puddle forming on Greg's belly. Greg bites his lip, and squirms.

"Fuck, please," he whines.

Heat flares in my gut and between my legs. My painted nails sink into the padded armrests, anchoring me to the chair when I ache to throw myself on the bed and rip off my clothes. To be consumed by warm skin and heat and eager hands.

But not quite yet. The anticipation is delicious. And my men are too good together. Dev is an expert at edging Greg into a begging, throbbing mess.

I fucking love it. I could come from watching them together. No touching required.

Dev tickles Greg's cock again, the angry purple head weeping more fluid onto his soft belly. His balls are tight to his body, the muscles of his thighs quivering against Dev's knees.

"Please, *please*," he breathes.

God, he's so close already.

I clench my thighs together with a little quiver of my own.

"Our delicate butterfly needs our attention." Dev's voice lowers to the husky, hungry tone that chases fire across my skin. "Look at her."

Greg turns his lust-drunk eyes on me, and it's all I can do not to launch from the chair. It would only take my mouth on his dick and one, slow suck to have him sobbing my name and exploding down my throat. Or maybe I'd tease him some more. Have Dev cage him against his body and glide his cock in the crack of his arse, edge his greedy little hole, while I kissed and licked and nibbled him into a frenzy.

Jesus, *I'm* close.

Dev runs his big palms up the inside of Greg's thighs, so near to the straining flesh at his core. Greg's eyelids flutter shut, unable to hold my gaze.

"Help me to please her and I will fill you where you ache."

Dev massages his thumb below Greg's balls. Greg spasms on the bed, his guttural cry loud enough to echo.

"Christ... man... *yes*. Fuck," Greg pants, tossing his head. "Steph?"

"Yes, prickles?" I say, my voice a tad breathless.

"Have I died and gone to heaven?"

"Not yet." I smirk. "But if you're a good boy, you will in about ten minutes on Dev's humongous cock."

Greg groans. He rolls onto his side and flops off the bed, with Dev's help. My two men crawl towards me. The sight of their arousal, their wicked intent, kicks my heart rate up a notch. My pulse pounds in the hollow of my throat. Dev's glorious wings arch from his shoulders, swaying gently with his graceful movements. Greg reaches me first. He places his tattooed hand on my knee, the lines of the spiderweb dark against his skin. Dev curls an arm around the back of my calves and tugs my arse to the edge of the seat. I swallow a gasp.

Greg manages a smug lip curl. "Ten minutes seems generous."

Fingers peel the clothes from my body. Mouths caress the

revealed skin and hollows. Tongues brand the faded scars beneath my breasts, working in perfect synchrony and setting my nerves alight. I writhe beneath their touch, tasting my heartbeat and them—weed and blueberries.

Ambrosia.

Together, they hook my legs over the armrests and leave me totally exposed. My muscles clench at the sweet expectation. My skin feels swollen and ready to burst, all my hairs standing on end.

"So lovely," Dev breathes, close enough for the hot air to lap my hole, eliciting another, heavenly clench of muscle. "So ready for us."

"Hold yourself open," Greg growls.

"Christ, prickles," I pant, but I obey. I'd be a fool not to.

I grab my shaking knees and spread myself wider. They share a glance and bend their heads—brown and blond—to nuzzle my inner thighs. My chest heaves, my breaths speeding as they inch closer to the aching core of me. They pause as one and roll their eyes up to where I strain and shiver above them. Their hair tickles my legs.

"This position does not hurt?" Dev says softly.

"Fuck, no. Don't stop."

Greg grins at my explosive exhale.

He's not the only one who turns into a mewling puddle under Dev's masterful touch. Both of us have seen Valhalla.

Another glance. A weighty, luscious pause. Hot mouths connect to my flesh. Pleasure zaps to my centre and rips a moan from me. They suckle and lick, their tongues duelling as they kiss each other and my desperate cunt between them. The sloppy sounds push me towards nirvana. I rock my hips, the orgasm building, heady and unstoppable.

I whisper their names, over and over, with a lot of begging and nonsense words, my voice climbing as the climax barrels towards me.

Tongues dip and swirl. Hot suction catapults me higher. I jerk in the chair, my muscles rigid. I hold my breath. Two fingers slide inside me and I scream my bliss at the ceiling. A tongue follows. A searing mouth sucks hard on my clit.

I lose track of my body. My men. There's nothing but sensation blazing through my consciousness to leave me limp and spent. And throbbing.

Fuck. *Me*.

I may be the one who's died.

Gentle hands coax my legs from the armrests into a relaxed position. A cheeky tongue swipes up my twitching hole, pulling a yelp from my throat.

"Definitely still alive," Greg chuckles.

I crack open one eye. My men kneel at my feet with shiny lips and smug smiles. The tenderness on their faces blooms another kind of warmth in my stomach. Just as precious.

"I love you both," I murmur.

Dev kisses my knuckles. "And we love you, delicate butterfly. Will you marry us?"

"God, yes," Greg blurts. "I want to fuck on the priest's desk like Maia and Hunter."

My heart stops, then thuds harder. I blink at Dev and Greg, each holding one of my hands.

Greg's eyes widen. "I mean, that's not why I want to get married. The dirty church sex. Or the sex, though it's goddamn awesome. I love you. I love Dev. I..."

My air locks in my chest, taking my words with it. My vision blurs and burns.

"Oh, fuck—Steph, say something. We shouldn't have done this when we were naked right?" Greg slaps Dev's bicep. "We should've waited til tonight like we planned. Not after sex. Oh, god, we ruined it."

Dev's mouth turns down in a sad pout. "She will not marry us? Did I do it wrong? I am sorry, my prickly pear. I got impatient."

"Yes!" I squeal.

Dev cocks his head. "Yes, we ruined it?"

"No, you sexy idiots. Of course I'll marry you."

"Well, you could be more romantic about it," Greg sniffs.

I burst into messy tears and hide my face in my hands.

"Shit, I was joking," Greg says, sounding panicked.

I laugh through my sobs. Dev coaxes my hands from my face. "You are happy?"

"Happier than I've ever been," I say, my voice choked. "Is it even legal?"

"Pretty sure it's not illegal to be happy." Greg scuttles, nude, to my dressing table opposite the foot of the bed. The bulbs bordering the mirror are off, two candles burning on the polished top surrounded by my many bottles and potions.

"Not happiness, prickles—marrying more than one person."

Greg rifles through the clothes piled on the stool. "Oh. Probably not. But we're rebels and saviours now, so who gives a shit?"

"I respect your human laws, but not on this," Dev says, wiping the tears from my cheeks and licking them from his fingertips. "We will marry."

Greg shuffles back to us on his knees and opens a tiny, velvet box. "Sorry. We did this the wrong way round."

I dab at my nose. "You did it perfectly."

Clasped in more velvet, the ring is a fragile band of silver inlaid with five stones: a diamond in the centre flanked by pink tourmaline and sapphire.

My gaze whips up to the men kneeling at my feet.

"Trans pride," Greg whispers.

My throat closes. More tears spill to soak my cheeks.

When it was just me and Dev in a relationship at the start, right after the apocalypse, I explained to him what a trans woman was and all the surgeries I'd had. I'm not sure he quite understood, having nothing in his culture to compare it to, but he told me he would have loved me whether I had multiple sex organs or none. It didn't matter as long as he had me.

I drop onto my knees, no pain thanks to my recent treatment from Bronwyn's magical shroud. Dev holds my shaking hand steady. I cry not-so-elegantly while Greg slides the ring onto my finger, then grab him into a hug and pepper his face with kisses and tears and, okay, probably a bit of snot. Dev wraps his arms and wings around us. Greg and I turn in sync to nuzzle his throat and jaw and cheeks. We press closer, gliding skin to skin. I taste myself on their lips.

"You made Greg a promise," I murmur into their mouths. "And I have been thoroughly pleased."

Greg shivers against my side. Dev smirks at him, his eyes filling with a heat that flares in my gut.

"Now I want you both above me," I say.

Dev directs his smirk at me, and the heat spreads outward.

"Whatever our delicate butterfly desires," he purrs.

He tosses me and Greg onto the bed. We both squeal, though Greg tries to hide his with a manly cough.

"You're fooling no one, prickles," I say.

He wrinkles his nose and flips me onto my back, blanketing

my body with his and claiming my lips to swallow my giggle. He licks inside my mouth, his hands buried in my hair, careful not to pull too hard on my wig. His erection swells against my stomach.

He breaks the kiss on a shuddering gasp. "Oh, Christ Jesus."

I peek over his shoulder. He drops his forehead onto my collarbone, his scorching breath washing over my nipple. Dev kneels between Greg's legs and mine, his big hands palming Greg's arse cheeks while he laves his crease. Greg twitches at each lap of his tongue.

"You better prep our boy good, blue bear," I say past the pulse thudding in my throat. An answering pulse throbs between my legs. "I want you to go deep. I want you both so deep."

"Fucking hell," Greg sobs into the curve of my tit.

Dev circles his rim with the tip of his tongue, then probes inside. Greg groans and thrusts his hips, rubbing his dick into my stomach. I wind my arms around his slick back and hold him tight.

"No friction until you're inside me," I whisper in his ear, my eyes locked on Dev licking him out. "And he's deep, *deep* inside you."

Greg whines, his hands tangled in the sheets. But he's not the only one who's frantic. It takes all my willpower not to grind my clit against him and release the pleasure swelling beneath my skin. Dev's wingtips tickle our ribs, amplifying the sensation. He slides a finger into Greg's hole alongside his tongue, and we both cry out. Greg starts to plead, then babble as a second finger joins the first.

"I'm ready," he chokes into my boob. *"Please.* I can't— I need…"

I grin at Dev over Greg's heaving shoulder. Dev's eyes sparkle between the globes of Greg's arse. He pumps his fingers and tongue another couple of times, eliciting a tortured wail from Greg. Dev surges to his knees and swipes the lube from the bedside cabinet. He slathers it on his cock and holds the bottle out to me. I release Greg to take it, and Greg props himself up on quivering arms, his head bowed.

He mutters, "Fuck, fuck, fuck," over and over.

He looks amazing when he's all sweaty and dishevelled and aroused out of his goddamn mind.

Greg manages to raise his gaze at the squirt of the lube into my palm. He bites his lip when I widen my thighs and rub the cool liquid liberally inside and out, unable to stop a moan at the glide of my fingers over sensitive flesh. I wipe the rest on his no-doubt-aching dick. He groans and screws his eyes shut.

"No coming until after Dev," I say.

"Oh, god, I love you, but I also fucking hate you a little." His eyes snap open and dart wildly. "No, wait. I mean—I love you. I love this. It's awesome. It's torture. Fuck, Dev, put me out of my misery."

Dev's fingers wrap around Greg's hips. "Always, my prickly pear."

Greg sheaths himself inside me with a tormented sigh. I wrap my fists in his hair and lean up to kiss him, groaning at the sensation of my muscles clenching around him. Dev's weight settles on top of us, pushing him deeper.

I know our angel has breached him when he hisses an agonised and devoted, "Oh, fuck—*yes.*"

Dev's thrusts roll him into me. I time my own so that our hips meet with Greg in the middle, utterly buried and filled. All he can do is hold on to the covers and shiver and take it. My stomach tightens. My swollen clit rubs deliciously against his pelvis. And Dev drills us all closer together.

"Dev, hurry," Greg pants. "Dev…"

He grunts Dev's name on every surge of our angel's hips. Dev tosses his head back, the cords in his neck straining. His big, muscled body spasms. The sight and sensation are too much for me. My orgasm rages through my nervous system, arching my spine and flailing my limbs. Greg makes a noise somewhere between a scream, a curse, and a prayer. I feel him flooding my insides, on and on and on, until he collapses on top of me, his body limp, scorching, and slick. Dev slumps over him, squashing us both into the mattress. My favourite place to be. I float on a cloud of bliss, barely conscious and totally euphoric.

I wonder, quite vaguely, if Maia is having as much fun.

8

Rain plasters my hair to my skull and runs in icy rivulets under the collar of my sodden hoodie. I almost wish for the frost of the morning, not this deluge from leaden clouds that rushed to gather as soon as Curran said it was time to begin our fitness training. I'm somehow both freezing and uncomfortably hot.

I enjoyed the gun tutorial. I divided my angels into groups and we were split between different classrooms at Dreghorn and the nearby Redford Barracks, since there are thousands of us. A little blip of worry tried to surface at the thought of them being out of my sight with a strange instructor. Then I remembered they were killing machines crafted by an ancient race. They've travelled to worlds beyond my comprehension to punish entire civilisations. They've endured the cruel hand of their creators and their own brethren.

They'll be just fine.

Haile taught our group—me, Hunter, Uziyah, Abayankari, and the Jewels, plus over a hundred of the favoured Protectorate. We sat in a tiered classroom, crammed into seats made for smaller, wingless creatures, and watched a screen while Haile described the different parts of the KS-1 rifle and how to assemble and disassemble the weapon. We also learned about the handgun—or small arms—carried by the British Army. A

Glock 17. A black, blocky thing that holds seventeen rounds and is surprisingly light.

Haile let me play around with one. Okay, she asked who wanted to, and I stuck my hand straight up while the rest of the angels stayed stoic and still. I may have waved my arm a bit. I held the gun for two seconds before I managed to drop the magazine on the floor with a clatter. Unlike her smirking superiors, she gave me a fond smile, scooped the magazine from the ground, and handed it back, showing me where the various catches and levers were.

Hunter always told me I couldn't fight another angel with a sword. They've trained to handle bladed weapons their whole lives. But guns are the great leveller. Not that I'll be fighting angels with guns, either.

"Pick up the pace, Buckthorn!" Curran yells from his dry position under an umbrella on the edge of the trampled field. He shakes his head at the stopwatch clasped in his fist.

He's lucky I have no air to tell him to bugger off.

My breaths saw in and out of my lungs, and taste like blood. Each exhalation puffs sticky moisture into my face, mixing with the chilly rainwater. My heart pounds against my ribs, the rest of my muscles spasming me into a gait that resembles the jerky movements of a broken robot.

"Do not listen to him, Maia," Hunter says beside me, breathing easily and loping along as if he could run forever. "You are doing fine, for a human."

I show him a weary thumbs up, no energy for speech. Mud splashes my shins and squelches under my filthy boots. Hunter's black hair flops in his eyes at each step, his clothes moulded to his broad chest and flat stomach. Water pours from his hunched wings. He catches my gaze on his collarbones and the droplets beaded there, framed by the laced collar of his top.

My mouth dries despite the abundance of fluid falling from the sky and pooling on the ground.

"When we are finished here," he says, his lips curving into a smirk, "I will need to wash you thoroughly. With my tongue."

Gulping, I find some hidden reserves and piston my legs. Curran scowls as I sprint past him. It buoys me for a few metres until the assault course emerges from the lashing rain.

I've lost count of how many times I've scrambled and swung and crawled through it.

I grit my teeth and throw myself at the rope net, tangling my limbs in the stiffened mesh. A furtive flap boosts Hunter to the wooden bar at the top of the triangular frame.

"Cheater," I gasp.

He grins, and I haul myself upwards, shaking like a baby monkey learning to climb.

When Curran described what our fitness training would entail, I told the angels they weren't allowed to use their wings. We all had to cover the course on our own two feet. And our hands. And twice on my face.

The net bounces beneath my cramping fingers. Hunter's grin melts to his arrogant expression, but Uziyah's grin more than makes up for it.

"Come, feeble creature, you are lagging behind."

Muscles bulge and flex as he scales the rope, barely out of breath. His blond hair is plastered to his bare back, his trousers sopping and sitting low on his hips. Obscenely low. Abayankari leaps to the apex and crouches opposite Hunter, her wings arched against the downpour. She looks like a gargoyle, except beautiful and shining white.

They've lapped me at least three times already—them and

the rest. They seem to be enjoying themselves.

Bloody warrior angels.

They pour around me again in a wave of power and grace, flowing over the frame and continuing on to the horizontal bars, leaving me, Hunter, Uziyah, and Abayankari on the net.

"We can help to improve your stamina." Abayankari's turquoise eyes scan my sprawled figure and my blanched fingers clutching the rope to stop me from tumbling to the muddy puddle at the bottom. "In ways you may find more pleasurable."

My eyes widen while I attempt to suck in enough air to speak.

"*Mine*," Hunter growls, glaring through the dripping cage of his hair. His wings spread, a great, black raven to Abayankari's swan-like feathers.

She smirks. "You can come, too."

Uziyah and Hunter share a competitive look, sizing each other up. Abayankari's hungry gaze flits between them.

"No one touches Maia but me," Hunter says.

"I am sure the feeble creature can choose for herself. That is a perk of their society, is it not?"

"Hunter. Is it. For me," I croak. "We—"

"Buckthorn!" Curran hollers, and I flinch. "Keep it moving. You have two circuits to go."

Oh, sure. Shout at me and not the three warrior angels also tarrying on the net.

I hook an arm over the next rung, and wobble higher. Dampness puckers my skin and pools in my lungs.

My phone rings, earning another flinch. I peel one hand free, and creaking fingers hook it from my inside pocket. I expect Steph's name, but 'unknown caller' shows on the screen under a layer of moisture. Sweat or rain. Probably both.

"'Lo?" I say through a violent shiver that threatens to toss me off the rope.

"What the hell are you doing, Buckthorn!" Curran barks, his voice approaching. "You don't take personal calls on *my* time. Give me that phone."

"I'm. Very. Important," I wheeze.

"Mrs Buckthorn? It's Doctor Muldoon," says the voice in my ear.

"Who?"

"Yannis. From the Roslin Institute."

"Right, sorry. What's—"

"Hang up this instant and hand it over."

Curran plants his fists on his rectangular hips and frowns up at me, oblivious to the puddle sloshing around his boots. Water drips from his cap. His discarded umbrella rolls along the edge of the field. I miss Yannis's next words.

"Give me the phone, Buckthorn."

"Ssh," I hiss.

Curran's mouth flaps.

"Is this not a good time, Mrs Buckthorn? I am afraid the news cannot wait."

"No, you're fine. Go ahead, Yannis," I say, finally able to breathe again. Multiple wings shelter me from the rain. Hunter, Uziyah, and Abayankari balance effortlessly on the apex beam while I cling to the net, shuddering as the cold seeps into my bones.

"I am your commanding officer," Curran splutters. "You do not *shush* me."

I wave my hand at him, scattering droplets.

"I just got off the phone with Doctor Alisand," Yannis says, his sentence punctuated by a slurp of tea. Is the man made of chamomile? "You are my next call, before I alert the GPA. I'm sad to say we've all lost the bet."

I stick my finger in my ear to muffle Curran continuing to list off his credentials. A flutter and squelch announce the arrival of the rest of our training group, having completed another circuit while we've been dawdling. Curran halts mid-sentence. The warriors gather around the net in a circle of upturned faces. Steam drifts from their bodies and mixes with the rain.

"They've used more tricks than we were anticipating. We extrapolated we would catch their infrared signature, especially when they started decelerating. Of course, we've relied heavily on the data gathered when you piloted the spaceship to Earth—what is likely to be visible and when—and from our study of the shuttles on the ground. We assumed they would approach in the shuttles, perhaps follow in the ship as they did before, but they used some kind of cloaking device, which is why they were not seen when they entered or left the Oort Cloud." Yannis chuckles. "Very sneaky, I must admit."

Goosebumps prickle my shoulders. "What the hell are you telling me, Yannis? The Creators are in our solar system? But not in the shuttles?"

Every warrior angel seems to stop breathing. Curran pulls off his cap and swipes an arm across his forehead, blessedly mute, for once.

"Our telescopes have recorded no sign of any shuttles. This time, they are coming in their ships."

I choke on my saliva.

"*Ships?!*" I squeak.

9

People cram into the meeting room in Dreghorn Barracks. Hunter and Dev clear a space, his two horny sidekicks flanking me to claim the chairs we had before, opposite Curran, Reynold, and Haile. Uziyah and Abayankari loom behind a seated row of military personnel. Their smug expressions confirm it's purely to make the gathered men and women uncomfortable. Yannis disappears amongst the bulkier bodies around him, though he still has a steaming mug of chamomile tea perched on a tiny corner of available table surface. Did he bring it from Roslin? A screen takes up one wall, showing the faces of GPA officials and world leaders or their aides taking notes if they weren't able to dial in themselves.

The weight of all that power suffocates the room.

Quite a few of them heard me shrieking over Steph's engagement ring. I nearly dislocated her finger so I could peer closer at it. The band suits her perfectly—trans colours and precious stones. I forgave her for abandoning me yesterday since she told me all the filthy details of the proposal. And I can't fault the happiness glowing from her face and the faces of her men.

I knew they were made for each other.

Curran raps a knuckle on the table. "Let's bring this meeting to order, shall we?"

The shuffling and chatter die immediately. I stop fidgeting with the command hub on my wrist.

"Doctor Muldoon, why don't you summarise what we know for the benefit of everyone here?"

Yannis pops upright, though he's not much taller on his feet than those seated around him. A precise finger neatens his already neat moustache.

"Our monitoring telescopes have identified six Protectorate vessels en route to Earth. Calculations project they will reach our orbit in eight months."

Yannis slides into his chair and takes a congratulatory sip of tea.

Curran blinks. "Thank you for that concise summary, Doctor. What are we likely to expect from these ships?"

Yannis looks at me. Slowly, the rest of the packed room follow his gaze.

"If they repeat the pattern of their first attack, they'll park their ships amongst the planets and send their shuttles to the ground," I say. "The Creators will command from the safety of space."

Salam and Tallai rarely got their hands dirty. They programmed their weapons—their *tools*—to do the hard work while they watched from afar, smug and righteous. Have they commandeered one of the other ships? The Creators in charge of the warrior angel faction are the overseers of each province of the Protectorate. But I stole their army, though they have plenty more warriors to send to subdue us.

If the angels are the favoured form, what do the rest look like? Hunter said the Creators built whatever creature was required to avoid an immediate response from the misbehaving civilisation about to be punished for abusing their world. But since the creations rarely mingle, he has no idea what form that may be. Uziyah has seen things that look like slugs.

Reynold smacks his fist into his meaty palm. "Then we will take the battle to them. Blow them to smithereens between the stars."

"Foolish human," Abayankari scoffs. "One on one they would destroy you, and they approach with six."

Sixty thousand warriors, each ship a different creation. Against our army of just over seven thousand. It's so much worse than six against one.

Curran would scowl at my dismissal, but the military never did much good before. This will be the first real test of the iron bullets.

Reynold huffs a breath. He starts to speak, cuts himself off, then shifts in his seat.

He definitely wanted to call Abayankari 'girl'. She would rip out his moustache in one clump, and shove it down his gullet.

I kind of wish he would, just so I could see it.

"It would not be one on one, or one against six. Nine shuttles from the Protectorate craft have been modified by NASA into fighting ships. We've also upgraded our satellite defence system and fast-tracked a ground-to-space missile programme." Reynold crosses his arms and leans back in his seat. "We are a force to be reckoned with. They will not set one foot on our soil."

I have to admire his confidence, misplaced as it is. We may have all of those things, but we only landed on the moon this century, for goodness sake. We watch, we explore. We have zero experience with space warfare. Salam and Tallai will laugh their grating laugh and blast them all to molecules.

"Then why were you so adamant about leading the warrior

angels?" I direct at Curran.

"You are the back-up plan," he says, "should an enemy breach our interstellar defences and enter our atmosphere."

"One slight problem with that."

Curran cocks his eyebrow. "Pray tell, Buckthorn."

"We don't want to slaughter the Protectorate."

Reynold bleats a laugh, earning him a glare from Haile. Incredulous murmurs swell through the room. Various languages mutter from the delegates on the screen.

"And why is that, Mrs Buckthorn? I doubt they are descending en masse to give us a stern talking to. If you hope to petition for peace, you'll soon be turned to dust."

Back to being Mrs Buckthorn. As if it's an insult.

Someone titters at the rear of the room, hidden by the press of bodies. Uziyah swivels his head and the tittering stops. Steph's face is thunderous.

I answer before she starts calling people names, keeping my voice calm. "Salam and Tallai are the overlords of one province. The Protectorate policies the *universes*. They have an infinite army. What do you think they'll do if we destroy one province's worth of creations?"

Silence falls. Anxious glances pass around the room. Rapid keyboard tapping drifts from the screen. Yannis takes a placid sip of tea.

"Are you telling us to accept our own destruction?" Curran says. "That resistance is futile?"

Hunter shifts behind me. I swallow an inappropriate giggle. His warm hand settles on my shoulder.

He told me resistance was futile when we first met. Then I stabbed him in the chest and sparked a rebellion that changed our fates forever. But it wasn't violence that saved us.

It was mercy.

I place my hand over his and squeeze his fingers. "No, but our survival depends on *how* we resist."

"Then what do you suggest?"

Steph catches my eye, her murderous expression lightening to her signature smirk.

"Christ, you want to adopt them all," she says.

I cough. "Well, not adopt. But they should be offered the same chance we gave the warrior angels—remove their cybernetics and let them choose how they want to live. The Creators are the only villains here. They're the ones who deserve to be punished." I spit out the last.

Salam sneered when he told me I would accept my punishment without any human scheming or Dev, cruel and unfeeling under the influence of a cybernetic collar, would maim Steph and Greg.

Let's see if Salam and Tallai take *their* punishment with fucking grace.

"What's to stop other provinces from sending their factions to kill us all and recapture their warriors?" comes a posh voice from the screen.

"Nothing, Prime Minister," I say, trying not to squeak. And failing.

"So it is futile," sighs the President of France, rubbing his weathered face.

Reynold jerks forward, his chest nudging the table and sending a slop of Yannis's tea onto the surface. A brief pout disturbs Yannis's calm. He removes a silk handkerchief from his shirt pocket and dabs at the offending puddle.

"We will not go down without a fight," Reynold barks.

Another voice from the screen—a heavy Iowa accent. "They

will roll over us like a farrowing pig."

"With all due respect, Madam President—"

"Couldn't we negotiate?"

"I say we hide. In bunkers this time."

I open my mouth, but my words are lost beneath the clamour. Black wings arch into my field of view, feathers brushing the people jammed around our end of the table.

"Be silent," Hunter growls. "Listen to Maia."

"The feeble creature knows what she is talking about," Uziyah says into the sudden quiet.

I roll my eyes. "Thanks, Uziyah."

"How could she possibly know more than us on the best way to respond to an ancient civilisation and their infinite army?" Reynold grunts.

Both Curran and Haile twist to look at their comrade.

About time. I'm getting a little tired of his attitude, myself.

"Because I asked," I say.

Reynold blinks at me.

"I asked the warrior angels," I continue. "Creations of that civilisation and members of the infinite army."

Reynold lifts his gaze to Hunter behind me. "What did they tell you?"

"Ask them yourself," I say, managing not to growl.

Reynold fiddles with the buttons of his uniform. He tilts his head at Curran.

Coward.

Curran folds his hands on the table top and raises his eyes to my husband. "How would you advise we proceed?"

"Listen to Maia." A burning glance sweeps to Reynold. "Mock her again and you will answer to me."

Curran's chair squeaks as he shifts.   "And what of the

Protectorate?"

Hunter maintains his intense stare until a bead of sweat dribbles into the scars on Reynold's cheek. "Six ships approach when they have ten left in the province. Four could be on assignment or they may have chosen to remain behind. If they were available, our Creators would have ordered them to come."

"How is he never as talkative with me?" Greg whispers, earning my elbow in his ribs.

"Are you saying it's possible some of the other Creators rebelled?"

Hunter nods at Curran. "It is possible. But if you destroy even a portion of the Protectorate, they will crush you. If you offer them freedom instead, and draw them onto your side, you may give the Creators pause from swift retribution."

"There are too many 'ifs' and 'mays' for my liking," Reynold says.

Hunter cocks a black brow. "There are no absolutes in war. Except death."

"How does it help us to stay their hand?" Curran says. "They could still decide to try and recapture every warrior we have. Or kill us all."

"If we are here, they will not use their planet destroyer."

"I bet it's a death star," Greg breathes, his eyes sparkling.

Steph rolls her eyes. "Here we go. Geek-out time."

I dig my nails into the thighs of my best friends, and lean forward at their yelps.

"Provinces are governed in isolation. The Creators are slaves to their reputation and would loathe any failure to control the systems under their charge. It would shame them in the eyes of their peers." I scan the faces of power in the room and on the screen. "If we rescue the majority of the Protectorate in this province, then we could convince the rest to leave us alone by threatening to involve other provinces."

"Did the angels tell you that?" Reynold sneers.

A snarl from Hunter has his face paling. He sinks into his seat. I pat Hunter's hand on my shoulder.

"Bronwyn told me most of it. I extrapolated the rest." I treat Reynold to an eyebrow arch. "Do you talk to anyone outside of your own little bubble?"

"Yeah, dickhead," Steph hisses.

Curran drums his fingers on the table, gaining our attention. "Let us, for argument's sake, agree that our goal is to steal the Protectorate, not destroy them. That means we have to let the shuttles breach our defences and land on Earth. We have to let sixty thousand highly trained warriors amass against us. How do we fight them—subdue them—without killing?"

I lift my arm and tilt my wrist outward. The screen of the command hub flashes under the lights.

"With this," I say.

10

Eight Months Later

The church is the same as it was almost three years ago for my wedding, though some of that time was spent in not-quite cryosleep. May sunlight shines through the stained glass to paint ruby and emerald shapes on the rows of pews, filled with Martello Court friends, our Jewels, and a few select Protectorate. Bronwyn dips her beak at me from the front where she sits next to Brigadier Haile, the only member of the army to be invited. Bronwyn's patterned wings and soft, grey skin show her young age.

The older the Creator, the darker and bonier they get, until the only colour left is the bright, cruel slash of their eyes.

In honour of the day, Bronwyn has chosen to wear a retina-sparing violet bodysuit instead of something more fluorescent. Her wings press against the wood of the bench seat. I return her nod from the back of the nave near the double doors into the antechamber.

Three people huddle nervously beneath the black-winged and sword-wielding angel statue above the altar. Well, two people huddle. The last watches me with a smouldering smirk that says he wants to steal me into the confessional and slip his hands under the turquoise silk of my dress. I press my thighs together, the iron knife in its sheath digging into my leg.

Another difference to my wedding—we're all armed to the teeth. My pretty bouquet of jasmine flowers, bluebells, and eucalyptus holds a knife buried in the core, the delicate handle patterned in gold and green.

A gift from Hunter for my last birthday.

Hunter's dark eyes travel from my chest to the split in my thigh, and heat everywhere in between. His wings flick, the blackness of his feathers complementing the tuxedo. A turquoise cummerbund matches my dress. There are no bulges beneath the cloth—ahem, except for that one—despite the multiple knives and the two Glocks stashed magically on his person, one of them mine. He rubs his thumb on the zirconium band around his finger. I touch my wedding ring, and send him a sultry smile of my own.

Greg and Dev huddle next to Hunter in tuxedos with rainbow cummerbunds, their pale faces both petrified and ecstatic. They have their hair tied in ponytails. Dev kisses the tattoo on the back of Greg's hand and a grin splits Greg's nervous expression. I hold up five fingers to them, and Dev's sapphire wings flare, almost knocking over a pot of jasmine on a marble plinth.

The whole church smells like Steph.

I clop on my heels down the short corridor past the confessional and into a square room at the base of the bell tower. Silk whispers on stone, the hem of my dress tickling the floor. Steph whirls from her perusal of her reflection in the floor-length mirror. The sight of her knots my throat and burns behind my eyes.

She's been ready for over an hour. I helped her get into the dress, for goodness sake. But she's still the most beautiful bride I've ever seen.

She smirks. "Are you going to cry again, Maia?"

"No," I sniffle.

Dammit.

White silk hugs the generous curve of breast and hip, then flares to the ground, offering glimpses of open-toed espadrille wedges. Pearl beads and intricate stitching decorate the lace bodice. A silver tiara perches on her chestnut hair that's styled like mine, loose curls framing her face. Precious stones mirror her engagement ring. The sun through the plain window highlights the subtle rainbow hue in the lace cape falling from her shoulders to form a shimmering train.

She's the gold at the end of that rainbow. Dev and Greg are going to faint when they see her.

We had to redo her makeup after I saw her in the full outfit and burst into tears. She joined me in the blubber-fest, though she seems to have forgotten that with the smirky face I'm being treated to.

I use the silk handkerchief attached to a bracelet at my wrist to dab my cheeks. Steph has thought of everything, no doubt based on how much she cried at *my* wedding.

"Everyone's in position. Except for my dad. No idea where he's wandered off to. I said we'd be another five minutes."

Steph nods and turns to the mirror, surreptitiously swiping a finger under her eyes. "What are our chances of being interrupted by the Protectorate like last time? They better not send ugly slug things, though I wouldn't be surprised if those bony dinosaurs crashed the wedding just to gloat."

"Nil," I say, smothering a shiver. "They're close, but they're

74

not that close. They won't skip past our defences unnoticed again."

"No, we'll just invite them through." Steph's reflection throws me a wry smile as she leans in to touch up her lip gloss.

Six dots appeared in the sky three months ago, as bright as stars. They slowly got bigger and brighter until they were visible during the day. Yannis explained that it's their engines we're seeing, pointed towards us as they decelerate rapidly on their approach to Earth.

"The defensive fleet are still going to harry them to make it look good," I say.

Steph rolls her eyes. "And get themselves blown to shit. Reynold really needs to calm his space boner."

Footsteps hustle towards us. Dad hesitates in the doorway.

I frown. "Aren't you supposed to be at the altar?"

His vestments sweep to the floor, unadorned but good quality. My dad—now self-appointed priest of his church, The Order of the Holy Angels. The minister at my wedding became a pile of dust under the haunting song of an arrow. We're continuing with our theme of unorthodox ceremonies, though. We may have had a massive cultural shift since the arrival of the angels, but group weddings are still not recognised by the Catholic church.

Just as well we have our own, and a sympathetic priest.

"Sorry to interrupt—" Dad stops, his gaze catching on Steph. The lines on his face smooth to awe. "Stephanie," he breathes, "you are a *vision*."

"Thanks, Mr Buckthorn," Steph preens.

As well she should. She's a goddess. Abayankari doesn't even compare.

"Please, call me John."

"Did you want to tell us something, Dad?"

He startles. The lines return to his face. Wisps of grey hair are all that remain on his head.

"Of course. Sorry." His eyes dart between me and Steph. His hands flutter on his vestments. "There are two people on the steps wanting entry. They say they're, uh, Steph's parents."

All the colour and happy light drain from her face. The sight of it sparks a fire in my chest.

No one is getting to ruin Steph's special day. Not even her family.

I guide a trembling Steph to a carved wooden chair. "Stay here. I'll deal with them. Unless you want to talk?"

Her rapid head shake nearly dislodges her tiara.

I give her a quick hug, and trot outside onto the wide steps of the church overlooking a narrow car park bordered by planters of bobbing daffodils. Dad scuttles at my heels. Two people stand on the sandstone slabs at the bottom of the stairs before it becomes the gravel of the car park.

"We want to see David," the man says.

The spark in my chest flares hotter.

"There is no *David* here," I snarl.

I can see the resemblance in Steph's father—the build, jaw line, and eyes. The mother has the same thin, brown hair. When Steph isn't wearing one of her fabulous wigs, of course.

"Maia, if there is a chance of reconciliation, perhaps we should—"

My head whips around, and my dad's mouth snaps shut. A curl of hair slaps me in the eye. I turn slowly to the intruding couple, the effort creaking through my neck bones.

"We are here to stop our son from committing polygamy and marrying an abomination. We demand to be let in," the father continues. "You should be ashamed for enabling this atrocity."

The freaking *nerve*. I doubt Greg is the abomination they're referring to. Of course they're transphobes and angel-haters. They abused Steph and kicked her out, leaving her homeless and alone at seventeen. She's thirty-three now, and finally happy.

"Your demands are not welcome," I say. "And neither are you."

Steph's undeserving father frowns at me. "This is a public space of worship. You can't refuse us entry."

"It's booked for a private event. You weren't invited."

His focus brushes past me to my dad in his priest's robes, then returns to me with a disparaging scan from my fancy up-do to my turquoise heels. I think about shoving my bouquet up his nostril, knife and all.

"You can't stop us," he says.

The mother remains mute, clutching his hand.

Steph always refers to herself as the glamorous assistant, content to stay in the background. But she was the one who gathered the Martello Court residents together during the apocalypse and built a fledgling communication network to contact more survivors using satphones while I was taming an angel. She's the one who never fails to unsheathe her claws against any threat to me. She is the foundation of my world. I wouldn't be here without her.

I straighten to my full height, not caring that it only puts me a couple of inches higher even when Steph's parents are at the bottom of the steps.

I've fought angels in hand-to-hand combat. Give me a gun and I can hit any target. These two interlopers are *nothing*.

"Try me," I say with a growl that Hunter would be proud of.

"I dare you."

I can't call Steph's dad a fruit fly, but I think about calling him a toxic transphobe.

Steph's mum fidgets, and drops her gaze to the sandstone. The dad opens his mouth, but his attention flies over my shoulder. He baulks.

Hunter's heat and icy scent roll over me. He steps up on my right side. Dev and Greg join me on my left to form an impenetrable wall. My dad inches towards the double doors, not one for direct conflict, though he had the balls to split from the Catholic church and host this radical group ceremony. Even my wedding to Hunter was unorthodox since angels weren't yet recognised as official citizens.

I look down my nose at the cowering couple.

Hunter and Dev's winged and scowling presence is probably more terrifying than mine, but I'm not mad they've come to help. We're all stronger together. Better.

"Steph doesn't want to see you. Leave now and never bother her again." I entwine my fingers in Hunter's. "Because *we* will stop you. Anytime, anywhere."

Steph's mum pulls on the father's hand. It takes two tugs, but they finally retreat. We watch them slink to their car and drive away with a crunch of tortured gears and gravel.

"Are you all right, Maia?"

I smile at Hunter and kiss his knuckles. "I am now." I release his hand and shoo the gathered men. "Right, all of you, back to the altar. There's a stunning bride who deserves her happily ever after."

"How stunning?" Greg grins. "I'm dying to see her."

I smirk. "Oh, you'll die for sure."

Hunter herds the rest into the church and down the central

aisle of the nave. I skip back to Steph, feeling like a knight who banishes dragons and narrow-minded bullies.

She folds me in a Parma Violet- and jasmine-scented hug. "Thanks, Maia. God, I hate how weak they make me, but I couldn't face them."

"And you never have to," I say. "Let's forget about those arseholes and get you hitched."

I straighten her tiara and fuss around her lace train until it sits to my satisfaction. She clasps her bouquet, a larger version of mine, to her chest.

"How do I look?"

I smile. "Like the most beautiful woman here."

Her lower lip wobbles. I wag my finger at her.

"Don't you dare," I say, unable to hide my hitch of breath as my throat closes again.

Her smile trembles, but she lifts her chin. "I love you, Maia."

I swallow. And again for good measure.

"I love you, too," I whisper.

She takes a step towards the door, grimaces, and stops. One hand fiddles at her thigh.

"Damn garter is pinching me."

"I'll get it."

I drop to my knees and duck under her skirt. Her giggle turns into a gasp.

"Christ, your fingers are cold."

I reposition the garter around her miles of creamy thigh. The silk holds four iron-blended throwing knives.

Steph with a firearm is a danger to every breathing creature, ally or foe. But she's as accurate with a knife as I am with a bullet. I should have known from when she stood on the esplanade of Edinburgh Castle and tossed a dagger, slicing open the cheek of a crimson-haired angel threatening me.

Persipha, the bitch.

I shimmy out from under Steph's skirt. "All sorted."

I lead her to where the short corridor opens into the nave, the murmurs of the gathered people swelling to the rafters. Skipping ahead, I send a thumbs up towards the altar. Greg's pulse is probably visible from the moon. The sweet piano notes and deep cello of Mozart's *The Swan* from *The Carnival of the Animals* fill the church. I dart back to Steph before everyone in the pews can rise to their feet and turn to watch our entrance.

I hold out my arm. "Shall we?"

She beams, and tucks her hand into my elbow. I walk my best friend down the aisle to her soulmates. Greg sways until an arm and a sapphire wing wrap around his shoulders. He looks like he's died and gone to heaven. Dev stares at his bride, his expression clear—pure adoration.

The joy in this one room gives me hope for the future.

Hope that, no matter what happens, we will triumph over the evil descending from the stars.

And they will wish for *my* mercy.

11

An unfamiliar noise drags me from an exhausted slumber to an aching body that could've done with another couple of hours of dreaming. Dreaming about black feathers stroking slick skin and clever fingers massaging my throbbing places. I glance at my phone on the bedside table, but the screen is as dark as the rest of the room, except for a soft glow blurred by my glass of water.

The past week since Steph, Greg, and Dev's wedding has been stuffed full of strategy meetings and training sessions. Steph and Greg got a couple of days off for a honeymoon of sorts. Dev had no luck. Of course, I kept quiet when he inevitably snuck off, though it's hard to sneak when you're a six-foot-three warrior angel with bright sapphire wings.

In between the tedious strategising and training, we also had psychiatric evaluations to ensure we're all ready for the war to come. The apocalypse dragged on for a month and a half after we fought back, and that was against the inhabitants of one Protectorate ship. With six, it could all be over in a few days when they crush us beneath the might of their armies. Or we hold them off long enough for my plan to succeed, then we make them regret they ever invaded our little blue planet.

I'm praying for the latter.

The sound vibrates again. It reminds me of the Creators' language—grating buzzes and clicks—except the translation fluid in my ears isn't forming it into words. So it's just a noise. An annoying, intrusive, unknown noise. Not someone speaking.

The mattress shifts beside me. Feathers whisper against the sheets.

"What is that?" Hunter says, his voice low.

His night-penetrating eyeballs will let him see that I'm awake, though he's a shadow in the blackness to me.

I sit up, the duvet pooling in my lap. Cool air teases goosebumps on my bare arms and beneath the silk of my nightie. My hand follows the gentle glow beyond my water glass, and scoops up the command hub. Dread swoops to my gut.

White text on a dark screen shows 'Incoming Call...' then the hateful name in all of its full and disrespectful glory: 'Salam'ac k'tai'moran.'

I tilt the screen at Hunter. My fingers tremble.

"He's phoning direct," I say through numb lips. "No way would Bronwyn forward his call without a warning."

Hunter gathers me into his body, my back to his chest, his feathers blanketing my arms and shoulders.

He surrounds me with heat and ice, and says, "Answer it."

I accept the call. Silence fills the room, as heavy as the weight around my heart. I brace for it, but still flinch when a voice penetrates the quiet, amplified from the command hub.

"Are you there, human? Are you listening?"

The English words overlie the buzzing clicks of the Creators' language without any lag. Instantaneous translation from superior technology.

Everything they have, everything they do, is superior. Why are we even trying to fight them? Why was I stupid enough to suggest it? As if we can possibly have a chance. We should just—

Hunter squeezes my ribs, reminding me to breathe. I suck air in slowly, though my lungs scream for it. Hunter kisses the top of my head.

"I want to speak to the human," Salam's awful voice continues. "The tiresome, meddling human who dared attack me in my own ship and stole Creator property. Bring her to me, so that I may hear her fear at what is to come."

I wet my lips and swallow hard to avoid croaking at him. He's had enough of my fear. Enough of my pain. The next one to suffer will be him, not me.

"What do you want, Salam?" I say in a calm and confident voice befitting the leader of several rebellions and the protector of warrior angels. Soon to be the protector of the Protectorate.

A hiss shivers out of the command hub and into my bladder. I tell myself I don't need to pee.

"My name is Salam'ack'tai'moran," he says, clacking his beak. "You will address me—"

"Call me Maia instead of human and I'll use your full name."

"You are a trifling waste of oxygen, *human*. I will do no such thing."

"Then, I say again—what do you want, *Salam?*"

My heart knocks against my breastbone and Hunter's encircling arms. Tension creeps through his muscles, turning his solid warrior's body to stone. A growl, not yet audible, rumbles from his chest to my spine.

"I want you to understand the fate that is coming for you. The fate you chose with your defiance." Air whistles from Salam's nostrils and into the speaker. "I would have spared your piffling planet had you accepted your punishment with the grace and quiet suffering it deserved. Instead, your human arrogance will herald the extinction of your destructive civilisation, and peace will reign once more within my province. You will be a blip, quickly forgotten."

My breath wobbles in, then slowly out. "Turn your ships around or be prepared for an embarrassing defeat. Your province will never recover from the shame."

I wince at Salam's choking, grinding cackle. Memories of him on the spaceship try to surface, but I squash them down. The effort of it shivers to my toes.

"You dare to threaten me?" Salam says, amused rather than angry. "You are weak, human. You are *nothing*. Your ignorance alone protects you from the full knowledge of what is coming for you. Six Protectorate ships against one planet is a historic force that will wipe the stain of humanity from the universes."

Hunter cradles my arm holding the command hub, his knuckles white, though his touch remains gentle. He leans forward, bending me closer to the screen. His hot breath blooms across my scalp.

"Where are the other four ships?" Hunter says, the growl now clear in his voice. "One as egotistical as you would bring all ten to bear, were that an option."

Five seconds of beak snapping and leathery flapping drift from the command hub, accompanied by the thud-thud-thud of my pulse.

"I had hoped the humans would fail in destroying your cybernetics," Salam says, utterly calm, "but I see you have been polluted once more by their weakness. No matter. We will re-programme you into the magnificent weapon you were, with shielded cybernetics resistant to interference. This has been an expensive but pertinent lesson for us all."

"Hunter is *mine*," I snarl. "You're never getting him back."

I stop myself from saying more. From telling him all the angels are mine. I imagine Salam waving a spindly hand, his fingers as multi-jointed as a spider's leg.

"You waste your breath in repeating yourself. I have reclaimed my property once before, and will do so again. But I will spare you the death you deserve beneath his blade and righteous fury. You will die unnoticed in the coming battle, and all of humanity will perish alongside you. I will transform your filthy planet into a wildlife sanctuary."

Another grinding laugh. It stops abruptly when Hunter asks in a soft yet menacing tone, "You did not answer my question. Where are the other ships?"

"I did not answer because you are a weapon. A *tool*. You do not question me. You obey."

Hunter raises my arm, pulling the command hub closer to his face. His wings bristle. Heat pours from his body. His hands are steady and strong where he holds my wrist.

"The days of our obedience are past," he says, his voice lower. Deadlier. "Take heed of this, Salam, and turn around as my wife suggested."

Salam splutters for a good minute at Hunter's use of his shortened name. I tangle my fingers in Hunter's hair and place a soft kiss under his jaw. He nuzzles me into the smooth curve of his neck.

"Wife! *Wife!?*" Salam spits. "You insolent creature. I will punish you until you beg me to return you to your former glory. All will bear witness to your shame. All will—"

"I, too, have a vow for you," Hunter says over Salam's

indignant squawking.

Silence fills our night-dark room. I picture Salam hunched over the command hub on his wrist, his beak close enough to graze the unit. A sharp-edged vulture in an area of screens with a silver-domed ceiling, his violet eyes narrowed to bright slits. Is Tallai next to him, listening? You hardly got one without the other on their ship. He was a shorter figure—shorter stature, shorter bony crest—but no less mocking or cruel.

Hunter's chest expands against my back. He holds his breath for another beat of heavy silence.

"You will die at my hand for what you made me do to Maia," he says, his words drifting as soft as a feather. "So bring your army, Salam. We have many more lessons to teach you."

12

Six Protectorate ships enter low Earth orbit the next day. Six bright shapes reflecting the sun and visible to the naked eye. Photos from telescopes and through binoculars flood the internet, offering more detail of the angles and lines of each hulking vessel. One site provides comparison shots of the alien crafts beside the International Space Station at the same magnification. The ISS looks like a minnow next to a whale.

Not that I need the contrast. I've seen them far closer than I ever wanted to.

I wait at the head of my warrior angel army, my face tilted towards the summer-blue sky. A gentle breeze shushes over the heather-clad peaks of the hills above the firing range at Castlelaw. Purple and cream flowers blanket the slopes descending northward towards Edinburgh, the castle just visible in the distant haze. To the right of it, Arthur's Seat looks more like an alien mushroom than a slumbering elephant with the spaceship parked on top of it.

Warm air caresses my cheekbones. Sweat gathers beneath my body armour. Quite different to the snowy Christmas day we took our first stand against the Protectorate. I have a comms headset stuck to my face instead of a walkie-talkie and my green t-shirt says 'The Commander' in bold white letters.

A present from Steph and Greg. Brigadier Haile chortled at it until a glare from Curran sent her scuttling to muster her brigade. Reynold is somewhere in the Roslin Institute to the east, directing our space defence via NASA and the other agencies. Yannis buzzed along after him like a joyful little bee, slurping on chamomile instead of nectar.

Curran is overseeing three brigades, including Haile's. All-terrain military vehicles and infantry pack the surrounding hills and access roads.

Do we look like ants to Salam and Tallai? Tiny insects, so easy to crush.

I grip Hunter's hand hard enough to bruise his fingers, but he doesn't complain. Warrior angels don't bruise. My other hand squeezes the butt of my Glock in its waist holster. A KS-1 rifle hangs past my hip on a strap.

"How long until they reach us?" Steph says on my right.

Throwing knives in a modified sheath criss-cross her chest and wrap around her waist. Her wig matches Dev's hair, and is tied in a pert ponytail that swings when she moves. A clear polycarbonate riot shield sits at her feet.

"Could be hours," I say. "Could be days."

"And we're just going to stay here and watch until then?"

Greg cranes forward to peer around Dev's muscular frame, both of them kitted out like me and Hunter and the rest of the angels. A riot shield is balanced on the heather in front of him.

"You can't possibly be bored. We're on the front line of saving the world."

"Been there, done that." Steph pretends to yawn.

I manage a smirk, though it feels thin and bloodless. Will this be the last battle I have to suffer through? The apocalypse was bad enough, but the events on the spaceship broke me. What if this fight is the beginning and not the end? What if it triggers a multi-universal meltdown where our sky fills with thousands of Protectorate ships, instead of just six?

"I like this human," Abayankari says on Hunter's left. "Would you couple with us? Uzi's feeble creature was not so keen. Unless you have reconsidered?"

Her white hair slithers across her shoulders as she bends to look at me, ignoring Hunter's growl. He twists his body to block her view, keeping a hold of my hand.

"I'm still good, thanks," I say, returning my gaze to the sky. "And you?"

"Uh…" Steph says, unusually speechless.

A masculine snort ripples from Abayankari's direction.

"She comes with the blue freak and his human puppy," Uziyah says.

I roll my eyes. "Still making friends, I see."

"It is what I do best."

"Thanks for the offer, but I'm fine with the freak and the puppy."

"Hey, now," Greg says.

"You do have puppyish tendencies, my prickly pear," Dev soothes. "You are cute and eager and you like it when I rub your belly."

Greg blushes to the roots of his brown hair, which is tied back with one of Steph's sparkly hair accessories. Or I assume it's Steph's. Greg has really settled into his own skin this past year.

My chest warms to probably the same temperature as Greg's face. I find myself smiling at the lot of them, from the offensive Uziyah and his scary partner to my best friends and my soulmate. Somehow, they make me happy even on the cusp of global catastrophe.

"Getting back to the standing around part," I say while Steph tickles a squirming Greg in the stomach. "We stay and watch and hope they take the bait."

And I'm the bait.

A command hub circles each wrist, similar to when I relieved Salam and Tallai of them on the spaceship, but without the mauve bodysuit held together by threads. I still have a knife up my sleeve. Bronwyn says the units have trackers for locating their owners across the universes. We're aiming to lure Salam and Tallai and their ships directly to our vantage point in the Pentland Hills away from human habitation. Having the warrior angels gathered at my back should also be a temptation they can't resist.

But who really knows how the Creators will react? It won't be a great start to our third resistance if they split up and slaughter a swathe across the globe, ignoring us. The GPA are ready to respond to such a scenario and protect who they can until we scramble to redeploy. There were plans to use our ship on Arthur's Seat as an enticement, but I definitely won't be setting one foot on it.

Much to Bronwyn's disappointment. She'll be in the room of screens right now, watching the news channels, waiting for serious casualties to be brought to her, since we didn't have the materials to replicate the healing shroud and tank of pink goo. I'd feel guilty about leaving her on her own, if she were on her own. She's been spending a lot of time with my dad since Steph's wedding. He was there this morning when she called to wish me good luck. They seem fascinated by each other. If it were to develop into something more, it would be... kind of sweet.

90

Dad's been alone a long time.

"Something is happening," Hunter says, dragging my attention back to the sky.

My hands tighten on my gun and his fingers.

"You may be the bait, but they will not touch you," he says in his protective, growly voice. "Never again."

I nod to show I've heard, and that I believe him, but can't pull my gaze from the perfect blue above us. Brilliant flashes leave white spots on my retinas.

"What is it?" I whisper to no one in particular.

"Explosions," Greg says grimly. "They have no sound in space. We might get debris if it's propelled into our gravity field."

"Speak English, prickles."

Greg wrinkles his nose at Steph. "That was English."

"Is it us or them—whatever's exploding?" I say, interrupting their affectionate bickering.

"Probably us," Greg sighs.

More bright flashes. More specks in my eyeballs. Streaks of flame and smoke fill the sky and paint lines to the horizon.

"And there's the debris," Greg says.

Steph shakes her head. "Well, Maia did try to warn them. Anyone else surprised the GPA's 'new and improved' satellite defence system defended diddly squat?"

A fireball the size of a plane whizzes above us, crackling and screaming. Three heavy heartbeats of silence, then a huge whump and the crunch of glass and stone as it impacts somewhere in Colinton. Black smoke purls towards the tainted sky.

So much for trying to avoid casualties in the city. The battle hasn't even started. Not for us, anyway.

Greg winces. "Nope."

"Are you sure they won't just shoot us with space lasers and take the annihilation of your faction as an acceptable loss?" I say.

"I am sure," Hunter says over Greg's snicker of, "Space lasers."

The brilliant flash of Reynold's overwhelmed defence getting blown to smithereens finally stops. Wispy trails mark the path of debris. We all scan the heavens. Sirens shriek towards the collision site.

"Maybe it was the Creators' ships getting blasted to bits?" Steph says, her voice a hopeful lilt.

"There wasn't supposed to be any blasting. Nothing too destructive, anyway."

"You can't save everyone, Maia," Steph says softly.

I swallow past the clog in my throat, but don't answer. She's right, though I will try. I'll try to save the Protectorate and turn the tide on the Creators, but not if it means sacrificing the ones I love.

I just wish we had a choice. A choice that didn't involve violence and bloodshed. But that's all the Creators understand.

"The Protectorate ships are advancing," Curran's voice says in my headset, somewhat belated. "Prepare for Phase Two."

I press the button over my ear. "Copy that."

The sky starts to boil. Sickly yellow clouds pollute the blue and fill with flickers of orange and red, like fire shrouded by mist. The eerie silence of it sends shivers down my backbone.

Until a sound builds. A roar. A tsunami of noise.

Shapes breach the roiling clouds.

"Jesus, man," Greg breathes.

13

Darkness sweeps across the empty streets of Edinburgh. The Protectorate ships eclipse the sun and turn the summer's day into an unnatural twilight. They hang in the sky—six monstrous, black shapes as eerily silent as the warriors they trained. Streaks and lines of light paint the surface of the hulking vessels.

"They are being intimidating," Hunter says.

I lick my lips and say, "It's working," at the same time Steph snorts, "No shit."

"How do they float like that, fighting against our gravity, without any sound?" Greg says, pinching his beloved in the ribs.

Hunter keeps his midnight-blue eyes on the ships.

"Technology," he says.

Movement flickers at the base of the two vessels in the middle. Pieces of sky shimmer and fall.

"And here come the shuttles." My words are hollow. Numb.

We lost good people in the apocalypse. How many will we lose today? Will I still have my friends around me when the sun sets, or will there be a gaping hole that one of them used to fill? Is this the battle where my luck runs out?

Perhaps we'll all be dead by sunset.

I tug on Hunter's arm until he looks at me.

"I love you," I say, my breath hitching against the pain in my chest.

He grabs my hips and lifts me into the solid heat of his body. I wrap my legs around his waist, his guns digging into my inner thighs. His thumb brushes my cheek and captures a tear.

"And I love you, Maia," he says, cupping my face. "I will love you to the end of your days, which will be many decades from now. Not here on this barren hill. Not under tyranny. Only time will conquer you, as it conquers us all."

My mouth collides with his in a desperate fumble of lips and teeth. I kiss him, taste him, like it's my last chance. My fingers tangle in his hair. I press myself as close as I can get without climbing inside him.

Greg sighs. "I wish he'd talk more. He's very poetic."

"Shut up, Greg," Steph says, "and bring those sexy lips over here."

My best friends make out like there's no tomorrow, no doubt joined by their third with the slurps and groans coming from their direction. Hunter shields me in a cocoon of his wings, and palms my arse, grinding me against his erection. My gasp rips my mouth from his.

He smirks at me. "When this battle is won, you get to pick your reward."

"My reward?"

He leans close, his hot breath tickling my ear and melting my brain. "You can do anything you want to me."

"Anything?" I squeak.

"Anything," he whispers, then kisses me breathless as well as mindless.

Oh, boy.

I picture him on our bed, his wrists and ankles bound to each corner. Naked skin gleaming in candlelight. Flickering shadows complementing his black hair and feathers and his dark, hungry eyes. I want to tease him. Have him at my mercy. Take him to the brink until he's a frantic, heaving mess beneath me. Until he breaks from his restraints, wild and untethered, and claims me like the savage angel he is. Savage, yet gentle.

"What are you thinking, Maia?" my savage angel purrs.

I swallow past my galloping pulse and manage a smirk of my own. "You'll find out when we win."

"I look forward to it."

After another squeeze of my arse, he slides me down the front of his body until my boots touch the heather. I turn my back on the shimmering shuttles descending towards a flat area of stunted gorse bushes near the base of our slope. Watching them makes me dizzy, anyway. I scan the faces of my friends and warriors instead, and aim my KS-1 rifle at the sky.

Once, it was a sword in an avenue of fallen angels and snow.

"Shoot them in whatever they have for a brain," I shout. "Then we take our fight to the Creators."

Steph and Greg whoop and brandish their rifles. The warrior angels don't cheer, but the fire of battle sparks in their eyes and shines from their bared teeth. I spin on my heel, my weapon dropping on its sling. Down the hill, twenty reflective shuttles settle into a long line and hover a metre above the ground. The grass dances beneath them. Yellow gorse flowers rip free and swirl away. I lift my gaze to the black ships in the sky.

Salam and Tallai are on one of them, eager to witness the carnage. No doubt expecting us to crumble in minutes beneath the strength of two Protectorate factions when they almost crippled our world with one.

But that was a long time ago.

I point my middle finger at the ships. "Fuck you, Salam and Tallai."

"Yes!" Steph hisses. *"Fuck them."*

Black openings gape in the sides of the shuttles.

And an army of nightmares spills out.

14

"Some worlds worship those things?" Greg says, a green tinge rising in his cheeks.

Uziyah's usual smug expression settles into serious lines, his focus on the creatures oozing from the closest shuttles. "In the Narthrax system, they were considered to be gods."

The warrior angels were often worshipped by the civilisations they were sent to conquer. Their form didn't provoke immediate hostility—until they started slaughtering the wayward planets, of course. It's one of the reasons why their faction is the favourite.

"Wait, is that the same galaxy as the oolingdan you talked about? The giant slug thing whose secretions smell like the rotten death of sedative gas?"

"There were many planets to tame in that system. Several ships were deployed, ours included." Uziyah's nose wrinkles. "I will never forget their stench."

Blobs of slime crawl from the gaping maws of half of the shuttles. Colourful organs slop and shift in the mass of transparent goo.

"Where's the fucking brain in these things?" Steph says, peering down the scope of her rifle. "They don't have a face."

I tap the screen of one command hub, swiping the view

around until it shows multiple dots, each one with an identifying number. Nothing registers within the shuttles themselves, not even the ones that haven't spilled their warriors onto the hills.

"I'm picking up the cybernetics, so they have a brain in there somewhere. Maybe it's that orb thing floating above their... I guess you could call it a head? Or dorsal lump?"

A circular object of dark material bobs above each creature. Eerie blue flickers at the core. A wave of sickness roils through my gut.

"Oh, crap, are they—"

A line of nauseating blue streaks towards me, horribly bright in the unnatural gloom created by the watching spaceships. I yelp and topple backwards, landing on my butt among the springy, scratchy branches. Hunter sweeps his wing in front of me. Something sizzles on his feathers.

"Soulreavers," he says grimly.

Steph and Greg leap to flank me, the edges of their riot shields clunking together to form a protective wall. The heather and slopes and blobs waver through the clear polycarbonate. The base of the hill has become a huge mass of jelly creatures slinking towards us. I scramble to my feet. Blue sparks skitter on the shields.

"Ray guns!" Greg grins over his shoulder in spite of the flashes of blue whizzing overhead. "We're living in *Star Wars*."

Steph rolls her eyes, hunched next to him. "Only you could get excited by weapons that'll turn us to dust."

"The arrows and swords were medieval and boring. No offence," Greg says to Hunter's raised brow.

Hunter's huge black wings flick, scattering sparks into the heather.

"Does it hurt?" I say.

Hunter smirks. "It is not as intense as the boring arrows."

I toggle my mic, opening the line to Curran and the other generals. "The first faction is slime creatures and they have soulreaving laser orbs. No movement yet from the other faction's shuttles. Commencing Phase Two."

At Curran's acknowledgement, I swipe a finger on the command hub, highlighting as many slowly slithering dots as I can. I raise my gaze to Hunter's dark and watchful eyes.

"Ready?"

He nods. "Always."

I suck in a breath. "Sorry, slime balls. There's no salvation without pain."

I tap the subdue icon that appeared as soon as I selected a bunch of the Protectorate. The slabs of goo slipping up the hill shiver and ripple. The hail of blue laser fire fizzles to nothing. Hunter's lips brush the top of my head. He launches into the air while the ghost of his kiss lingers. The wind from thousands of wings flattens the grass and rattles the heather. The dark sky darkens further. Steph, Greg, and I crouch behind our barrier. Gunshots clatter and echo among the hilltops. Bullets smack into the slime creatures and whine off the orb weapons, exploding several in puffs of fire and smoke.

I take a moment to witness the majesty of angels. They were impressive with their bows and swords. An almost unstoppable force. With a rifle nocked to every shoulder and their eyes narrowed on their targets, they are magnificent. Deadly accurate. My ears ring from the barrage of their bullets.

Steph's pointy elbow jabs into my sternum. "Less gaping, more commanding."

"Right, shit, sorry." I tap my ear. "Ready for extraction."

"Ground support incoming," Curran says.

"Tell the WAGS to bring a shovel," Greg snorts. "I'm glad I'm not the one who has to scoop up the goop. Do you think the Creators hump these guys?"

Steph shifts her shoulder against her riot shield and casts her eyes to the crowded heavens.

"Jesus, prickles," she sighs.

Warrior angels flap and hover, squeezing off a shot whenever the goo creatures so much as shudder. Jeeps and modified troop carriers crest the hills and converge on the stationary slime puddles, leaving tracks in the grass. Crushed gorse flowers scent the air with coconut. Sickly froth and silver slicks the surface of the creatures where the angels' bullets have penetrated. Black-uniformed soldiers jump from the vehicles. I expect their fingers to sink through the flesh of the Protectorate, but they seem solid enough when they lift them up and slop them into the back of the carriers, each one about the size of a sheep.

WAGS is the new name we christened the WACO teams, though they weren't enthused by it. It stands for Warrior Angel Ground Support, but was more commonly used to mean the Wives And Girlfriends of famous footballers and other high-profile sports personalities. The arm candy.

Greg thought it was funny.

The shifting ceiling of warrior angels blocks my view of the hulking spaceships. I scan the openings of the remaining shuttles while the battleground mills with people and vehicles.

What are they waiting for?

A flash of blue and a scream. A soldier half-way up the slope of our hill dissolves to pale dust and crumpled clothes. More flashes, more screams. I bruise my finger on the screen of the command hub. Iron bullets patter into the Protectorate. Organs swirl in the transparent soup. The first line of vehicles motors back up the hill, the sealed carriers flooding with sedative gas to keep their slimy occupants unconscious while they're whisked to the Roslin Institute.

After I made a fuss about their living arrangements, the angels were assigned to houses emptied during the apocalypse. Volunteers showed them how to cook and clean and look after themselves. Uziyah and Abayankari moved into the flat of the weepers and wailers below me and Steph at Martello Court.

I miss the weeping and wailing. The angels sound like they're trying to kill each other when they have sex. And they wonder why no one wants to join them.

Now, the huge underground room at Roslin has been adapted into a giant MRI. The squidgy Protectorate will be loaded inside and treated en masse to destroy their cybernetics.

Everything is going exactly to plan.

It feels too easy.

Dark shadows shift in the gaping maw of the shuttles. High-pitched shrieks send a spike of icy fear to my bladder. Steph and Greg meet my eyes from their braced position behind the riot shields.

"Do not like that," Greg says.

A shiny black wave pours, screeching, from the shuttles. Wicked talons rip into the soft earth and catapult bits of vegetation into the air. Four muscular legs propel the creatures past the shivering slime puddles waiting to be loaded into carriers. A long tail ending in a single spike arches over their backs. I glimpse huge fangs and three eyes, one on a stalk, before I swipe at the command hub. The new warriors fan out and gallop up the hill, aiming for the milling WAGS.

"Man, they're quick," Greg says, his throat bobbing.

Gunshots crack. A creature bowls into the heather, but claws itself upright and springs for the hill, muscles bunching, teeth snarling. A black tongue whips out.

"Uh, Maia… now would be a good time to stop them," Steph says, not looking at me.

I grit my teeth. "It's not locking on. They move so fast, and I lose them."

I jab at the screen. A tiny contingent of beasts collapses into the grass. Sweat drips into my eye. The creatures sweep closer, each yip from their fanged mouths jolting my heart.

"Oh, fuck," Steph gasps, dragging my gaze to the roiling hillside.

The wicked claws, teeth, and tail spike, the same black as the creatures' skin, glow blue. The colour streaks with the rapid churn of their feet and the angry gnash of their jaws. Their tails bob above their spines like the awful lure of an angler fish.

"Built-in soulreavers," Greg breathes with none of his joyful, sci-fi geekery.

My finger fogs the surface of the command hub. No sooner have I highlighted a clump of the freakish, panther-like beasts that they speed out of range.

There must be a way to lock them in. To select them all and keep them highlighted for the subdue function. The Creators wouldn't scramble and panic like this, struggling for control. They're all about control. Craftsmen who wield their tools without empathy. Who create weapons as merciless as they are.

I swipe the screen, but see no command other than the subdue icon that keeps flickering on and off when I lift my finger and lose my selection of the sinuous creatures.

"*Fuck!*" I hiss when the button disappears again right as I'm about to press it.

"Deep breath, Maia." Steph relinquishes her grip on her riot shield to squeeze my arm. "You got this."

But as I'm trying to calm my shaking hands and racing heart, the four-legged warriors reach the first of the soldiers still desperately trying to load the subdued Protectorate. A few black forms lie unmoving in the grass and heather from my paltry contribution and the precise gunfire of the angels flapping above us. The eerie blue of their pointy, soulreaving body parts fades to the black of their flesh.

A soldier strafes a line of bullets at an advancing creature. It twists in mid-air, dodging easily. Claws spear the dirt. Muscles bunch. The creature launches at the man and sinks its fangs into his throat. He dies on a gurgle, and puffs into dust. The beast shakes the powder from its three eyes, and leaps for the unprotected backs of two WAGS tossing a blob into a modified carrier.

I poke the command hub, a scream of frustration lodged under my ribs. The creature goes limp, barrelling into the WAGS and knocking them and the slime puddle to the ground in a tangle of limbs, talons, and gloop. Wounds froth along its spine. Bullets patter into its skull in a splash of silver.

"Incoming!" Greg yelps.

A tsunami of black shrieks towards us. Rifles clatter. Beasts howl and tumble to the ground, smothered by the clawed feet of their advancing brethren. Flashes of blue laser fire streak across the landscape as subdued slime monsters come to their senses and resume their slow, inexorable slither. Soldiers collapse into plant food. My heart lodges in my throat and makes it hard to breathe. Hard to think. The screeching of the mutant panthers claws at my brain.

Thudding feet and slashes of blue. Closer and closer. I swipe and tap. Swipe and tap. Curse. Creatures fall, but the rest keep coming.

Closer and closer.

"Buckthorn! What the hell is happening?" Curran barks in my ear. "My men are dying out there."

I mash my shoulder against my ear instead of using a finger to toggle my mic.

"This bloody thing didn't come with a manual. I'm doing my best."

"Your best is getting us killed."

Warrior angels fire their weapons into the unstoppable black wave. My ears ring. The air around us seems to heat with the proximity of the snarling mob. Many wingbeats stir it into a scorching wind that blasts my cheeks. My hair whips my skin in stinging lines.

I've examined every menu of the command hub. The damned device has limitless choices. It may be in English now, but it doesn't help when some of the options offer little explanation beyond a single word—shelter, sleep, protect. They could do anything.

And there's nothing to explain why I keep losing my selected area when the creatures move. I've had no cybernetics to practise on until now.

I use one finger to highlight, then subdue. Swipe and tap. Swipe and tap.

Salam and Tallai have multi-jointed digits on each hand. Maybe they used more than one to touch the screen. Maybe if I keep my finger on it—

"Maia!" Steph yells.

My head snaps up.

Mutant panthers crash into the riot shields, slamming Steph and Greg onto their backs and pinning them beneath. Blue claws gouge plastic. A creature snaps its jaws at Greg's pale face. Its fangs squeak on the flimsy layer protecting my best friend from a dusting. Its blue-tipped tail spears into the dirt.

"Leave him alone, you *Avatar* reject!" Steph snarls, trapped by her own creature, who sniffs at the shield separating them.

A sapphire blur scoops the beasts and tosses them down the hillside. Hunter drops onto another creature in mid-leap, driving its muzzle into the ground, his boots between its shoulder blades. His rifle shreds the top of its skull. Two mutants dive for him with claws extended, and his wings sweep them away. Gunshots batter the hilltop, careful around our frantic circle of fighting. Lines of blue sear my retinas. Dust swirls on the hot wind and grits my eyes.

Two beasts collide with Hunter. He staggers under their weight. Claws slice clothes and flesh. Bloodless wounds gape on his arms and chest.

"Hunter!" I gasp.

My finger swipes the command hub.

"Maia!" Hunter shouts beneath his cloak of talons and teeth.

A mutant panther sails for me, bringing death on the tips of its swirly blue claws.

15

The bullet from my Glock enters the creature's snarling mouth and pops from the back of its skull in a spray of black shards and liquid silver. Its limp carcass slams into me, and I join my best friends on my back in the heather. Claws skitter on my body armour and shred my t-shirt. I wait for the sting of a scratch, and dusty oblivion. My stomach clenches. My heart is beating so fast, it's a continuous thrum, muffling the noise of battle. The beast's head flops on my shoulder and bleeds hot and tingly blood against my neck.

My name is called in several voices that echo and blur together. I blink at the gaps of pretty cyan sky between churning wings and hulking spaceships. Soul-sucking blue lasers sizzle and streak like comets.

How the bloody hell did we get to this?

I shove at the body on top of me with one hand, my other cramped around my gun. Instead of the leatheriness I was expecting, the mutant panther's shiny skin is velveteen and soft.

"Maia!" Hunter's frantic voice climbs above the cacophony of rifle fire, snarling, and shouting. Curran buzzes angrily in my ear.

The weight on top of me doubles, crushing my ribs. A feline

head eclipses my view of the sky. It leans closer, peering at me over its fallen comrade and squeezing all the air from my lungs.

I've been here before. Pinned at the mercy of the Protectorate. Freezing grass. Rain, tinged orange by firelight, streaking past white-gold wings. Hunter occupied by fighting other warriors and unable to help me. Waiting for death as an arrow started to hum, the swirly tip aimed at my eyeball.

Except these creatures are twice as heavy as the angels. Solid muscle without the need for flying.

The beast sniffs at me. Delicate whiskers bristle from its snout.

"You don't need to do this," I wheeze. "Join us."

The creature cocks its head, pointy black ears pricked. Each eye is a different colour—amber, red, and pink, with a tiny square pupil and squiggly grey veins. The stalked one moves independently of the others and makes me dizzy.

"Let me help you," I pant.

Its muzzle wrinkles, baring soulreaving fangs as long as my hand. I expect drool and slavering, but its teeth look dry and horribly blue. Its ears press flat to its skull. A growl rumbles in its chest and spills from its mouth in a snarl. No words.

Maybe this faction of the Protectorate is not as intelligent as the others. Perhaps the Creators experimented with mindless violence, rather than cold and calculating.

I jam my Glock under its chin and pull the trigger twice. The creature's head jerks back and its body flops to the side out of sight. I wriggle from under the first beast and climb to my feet, gun in hand.

Our hilltop has been overwhelmed. Dev is a constant swoop of sapphire as he tosses mutant panthers left and right to clear a space around Steph and Greg. They huddle behind their riot shields, firing their rifles at the creatures thrashing in the grass and heather. Hunter stabs his knife into the head of a beast and drops it into the growing pile of motionless creatures at his feet. Black feathers dance on the wind. His top is in tatters, the skin beneath not much better, though there's not a scratch on his indestructible, laced trousers and boots.

I fire at a creature leaping for him, sending it rolling down the hill in reverse. Hunter's midnight-blue eyes meet mine and fill with relief.

Then horror.

I spin around, my gun up. Three mutants launch for me, claws extended. My finger twitches. One drops. The others are too close.

Shit. I'm dead.

A bulky shape thuds in front of me, bringing the scent of the sea and blocking my view of the leaping creatures. Flesh smacks against flesh. Snarls rip the air. Uziyah grunts, and his golden wings flare, bowling me back to my arse in the heather. Before I can even touch a command hub, a wave of black forces me to swap my Glock for my KS-1 rifle and spray the wall of advancing beasts. Yips and snarls and shrieks shiver into my gut.

Hunter fights his way towards me.

Dev defends his soulmates.

Abayankari dives and tears a creature from her lover's flesh. Uziyah drops to his knees.

I gasp his name, and scramble for him.

The remaining beast's talons are speared into Uziyah's broad chest while he wrestles to hold its snapping jaws away from his face. Bone cracks. Uziyah's cheeks pale, his teeth gritted.

His eyes are a circlet of sooty grey swallowed by the black hole of his pupils. He grabs the mutant's muscled forelegs, and his biceps flex. The thing braces its hind legs, claws furrowing the dirt. I aim my rifle at its temple. Abayankari darts in from the other side.

The creature twists its powerful body with another awful crack of bone, and yanks its talons free, dodging Abayankari. Uziyah groans and falls on his back. A bloodless cavity yawns in the centre of his chest, the edges ragged and prickling with shattered ribs. A silver lump slides from the panther's claws and tumbles to the ground. I land on my knees beside a heaving Uziyah.

Abayankari screeches, the sound more terrifying than the noise of the beasts around us. She leaps for Uziyah's missing piece at the same time as the creature. Her grasping fingers clutch at grass and soil as she skids across the ground in a tangle of white hair and ruffled feathers. The beast tosses its head. The object twirls into the air, shining like a lump of precious metal, then drops into the animal's waiting gullet. Tissue crunches between its sharp teeth. Its throat bobs as it swallows.

"No!" Abayankari shrieks. "You foul creature!"

She grabs the beast's snout from her prone position, using it to drag herself upright and slamming its jaw to the ground. She empties her rifle point-blank into its skull and reduces its head to frothy mush. Her knife flashes, stabbing into the creature's abdomen and gutting it from diaphragm to pelvis. Grey coils plop out. She hacks at a bright-yellow organ, then casts her knife aside to cradle a lump in her hands. It dissolves to sludge and drips through her fingers, nothing solid left.

Abayankari howls and raises her silver-streaked hands to the crowded sky.

I yank my gaze away and jab at the command hub. Rifle fire is all that stands between us becoming cat food and dust. I highlight every dot I can see, keeping one finger pressed to the screen while I use another to pan around. My thumb taps the subdue icon.

Silence falls on the battlefield.

16

"Uziyah," I whisper in the sudden quiet, "are you okay?"

My hands flutter over the ragged hole in his bare chest. His loose trousers are smeared with dirt and froth. His wings disappear into the heather, the feathers flicking at each heave of his ribs. His sunflower-yellow hair forms a halo around his head.

Half of his mouth ticks upwards in a smile. "No, feeble creature. The little bastard ate my heart."

The Protectorate's super-sealing ability ensures no blood loss from the arteries and veins around his missing organ. How long does that give us to get him to the medical ward in the spaceship on Arthur's Seat? A human would die within ten minutes if their heart stopped. Should I start CPR?

Abayankari thuds to her knees opposite me. Her turquoise eyes are the only colour in her face. She covers the wound in Uziyah's chest with her trembling, silver-stained hands. Her wings arch wide and protective.

"But, you'll be okay... right?" I swallow hard. "We can fly you to Bronwyn. Get you in the tank of pink goo. You'll be back to your antagonising self in no time."

Shadows stretch across our huddle. I lift my gaze. Hunter's sympathetic expression rips a hole in my chest to match

Uziyah's. Dev stands beside him, cuddling Steph and Greg, his face sombre. Greg sniffs, and bows his head. Tears well in Steph's eyes. Black-clothed WAGS scuttle in the background, loading creatures as fast as they can into the carriers.

I grip Uziyah's cold hand. "But... you can heal. You're indestructible."

"Semi-indestructible," he wheezes.

Abayankari presses her forehead to her hands in supplication. Her wings shake. A lump the size of Uziyah's precious, silver heart stoppers my throat.

I send Hunter a pleading glance. "I've seen your healing ability replace missing fingers. How is this different? It can't be different. He just needs time, and help."

"Maia," Hunter says softly, "we can heal missing limbs, but we cannot regenerate an organ from nothing. It would need some intact tissue."

My stomach clenches at the drying sludge stippling the ground and smearing Abayankari's fingers. My ribs contract, pushing my breath out in a sob.

"This can't be it. We have to do something. He can't die."

Hunter drops to one knee beside Uziyah's head, and places a hand on his shoulder. Uziyah tilts his face to meet his gaze.

"You were a worthy adversary," Hunter says.

Uziyah manages a smirk. "I still do not like you."

"The feeling is mutual."

Greg buries his face in Dev's pec. Steph stumbles a couple of steps to stand behind me. Her warm hand squeezes my shoulder and stays there. Tears blur my eyes.

Yips and snarls drift from the hillside, the slopes out of sight from my low position. A streak of blue zips into the hovering roof of watching warrior angels.

A panicked voice yells, "They're waking up!"

I swipe at the command hub. A tear drips onto the screen. Another tap quells the rousing Protectorate.

Does the subdue effect fade after a while, or is Salam cancelling my commands like he did on the spaceship when we wrestled with the sedative gas system? An important question, yet I can't find the strength to care.

"You're not allowed to die, Uziyah," I sob. "I forbid it. That's an order."

A chilled hand cups my cheek. "Do not cry for me, feeble creature. You gave me a taste of freedom, and it was everything."

I nuzzle his hand and weep into his palm. Abayankari raises her head. Fury blazes in her eyes, though her face is stricken.

"They will regret this," she snarls. "I will slaughter their worlds for you."

Uziyah touches his fingertips to her chest, to the place where his own heart has been stolen. His hand quivers.

"No, my love," he murmurs. "You must save them."

And then his strength, his personality, slides from his face to leave it slack and empty. His eyes flutter shut on a sigh. His hands flop to his sides, and my skin feels colder. Steph's tears speckle my t-shirt and join mine in the heather. Abayankari tips her head back and screams at the sky. I reach for her, but she shoves to her feet, her shining hair slipping through my fingers.

"Abayankari, wait," I croak.

She bares her teeth, her eyes dry and fever-bright.

"My name is *vengeance*," she hisses.

Her wings snap out and she throws herself down the hillside. We all scramble to the top of the slope. She swoops to the line of empty shuttles hovering over the gorse bushes. A dark maw swallows her whole.

"She doesn't know how to fly one of those things," I say, more a statement than a question.

Hunter shakes his head. "No, but she is smart. And motivated."

"Should we stop her?" Greg's voice is muffled, his face still pressed into Dev's chest.

The shuttle wobbles and jerks up, then down. It gouges a chunk out of the mud and gorse. The vessel scrapes sideways, then jitters back up. It spins around, the entrance still open, and zips into the sky, scattering warrior angels. They land as a unit and tilt their heads to witness. Several WAGS pause their extraction to follow the streaking path of the shuttle. The vehicle aims straight and true for the spaceship the mutant panthers came from. I wait for the Creators on board to blast the wayward shuttle out of the sky.

And wait.

Maybe their defence systems don't recognise their own transport vessel as a threat? You'd think, in their infinitely smug wisdom, that they'd have a manual override.

But, to paraphrase the Bible, pride comes before the fall.

The targeted spaceship turns slowly, the thrum of its engines loud enough to vibrate in my chest. I hold my breath. Abayankari pilots the shuttle full-speed into the hulking ship's undercarriage. The shuttle explodes in a fiery starburst of orange and yellow, the boom of it crackling across the landscape and echoing between the hills. Shards of reflective shuttle material twinkle to the ground, trailing smoke. The need to breathe aches between my ribs. The spaceship looms, as dark and intimidating as ever.

114

Please tell me Abayankari didn't sacrifice herself for nothing. She was psychotic under the influence of the Creators' cybernetics and only slightly less scary as her normal self. She wasn't a friend, but she made Uziyah happy.

Pain lances my heart.

Uziyah... How can the larger-than-life angel be gone? It's not fair.

None of this is fucking fair.

Something groans. My gasp eases the pressure in my chest. The Protectorate ship, a tiny part of it smoking and burning to mark the resting place of Abayankari, lists to the side. Engines whine. An explosion whumps from somewhere deep inside.

Such a tiny craft to damage a massive ship. Did she hit something vital, like the creature that stole Uziyah's heart? Knowing the exact place to strike to fell even the strongest of warriors.

The air ripples around the giant vessel. The ship continues to list despite the shrieking engines, and slams into its neighbour—one of the spaceships still containing a full contingent of Creators and Protectorate. Purple sparks skitter across the black surface and rain down, fizzling to nothing. Fire and smoke billow from the contact point. Falling debris sparkles and scatters. Metal screeches on metal. Both ships cant sideways and lose altitude in a slow arc, dropping from the line of four others.

"Bloody hell, are they going to...?"

The whistle of wind swallows my soft words. The falling spaceships pick up speed, growing larger as they plummet. The globes and streaks of light that paint the angular surface shine brighter, leaving afterimages in my eyeballs.

I'm holding my breath again. Gaping. I duck as the huge

115

ships scream overhead, locked together and heading south-west, away from Edinburgh.

Thank goodness. Pancaking the city would tarnish any victory we may have. Though I don't doubt there will be casualties.

Strong arms wrap around my midsection. Black wings boost us skyward, stealing my breath in a whoosh. The air fills with the flap of thousands of wings. Dev flies next to me and Hunter, Steph and Greg tucked under his arms. The sight of Uziyah's body, alone in the heather and dwindling in size as we gain height, is another punch to the heart. The warrior angels hover in tiers, watching the howling descent of the stricken ships. WAGS scramble like black ants below us.

They've cleared an impressive swathe of the battlefield, but I highlight and subdue the remaining cybernetics just in case.

After a final, grinding moan, the Protectorate ships crash to Earth with a ground-shuddering roar, flattening the rest of the Pentland Hills to our immediate south-west. The impact ripples outward. WAGS yell and topple, the surface kicking beneath their feet and tossing them easily. Troop carriers leap about a metre into the air. Alarms blare. Fire, dirt, and smoke billow above the downed ships.

"The Creators are going to be *pissed*," Greg says.

17

The sky is clearer with two Protectorate vessels smouldering in the craters that used to be a range of hills stretching twenty miles. The ships have collapsed in on themselves to reveal dark struts like the rotten bones of a giant monster. Helicopters buzz towards the crash site.

Will there be any survivors? The Creators, as advanced as they are, are as vulnerable as the rest of us. A smash like that may even be beyond the hardiness of the Protectorate. Nothing intact means nothing to heal.

Like Uziyah.

I tap at the command hub, Hunter's arm a steady band around my middle, pressing me to his chest. The flap of his wings slows, and lowers my boots to the springy heather. Dev settles beside us, relinquishing his grip on Steph and Greg. Hunter keeps me cuddled against the front of his body. The rest of the angels split between landing on the slope and staying in the air.

Cybernetics register at the crash site. It could mean some warriors are alive or the cybernetics are intact, but its host is beyond saving. I subdue them and the Protectorate scattered over our remaining hillside, then lift my gaze to the waiting angels.

"I want five hundred of you to go to the crash site and

search for survivors. Bring them back here for the WAGS to transport." I scan the shifting mass around and above, spotting the ruby wings and curly brown hair without needing to shout his name. "Markian, pick another to help you carry Uziyah to Bronwyn. He's... he's beyond healing, but put him in the ward until we can give him a proper burial."

A crowd of angels peels off and swoops for the remains of the spaceships. Markian bows at me. Watching him and another violet-winged Jewel carefully cradle Uziyah between them carves my stomach hollow. The bulky angel looks smaller in death. Hunter wraps his wings around me in a comforting cocoon.

I clear my throat. "The rest of you—except for Hunter, Dev, Steph, and Greg—help the WAGS clear the blobs and the panthers." At the curious head tilt of thousands of warriors, I amend that to, "The subdued Protectorate. And watch the sky. This isn't over."

Feathers rustle. My hair dances in the wind of their departure. Angels and soldiers swarm the hillside. Nineteen empty shuttles shimmer and hover in a line at the base, reflecting the sun.

"What about us, Boss?" Steph says, aiming for her usual smirk, though it's somewhat ruined by her scratchy voice and the tears still shining in her eyes. "Do you think those two vultures bit the dust on one of those ships?"

"Let's find out," I say.

I relay everything to Curran via my comms headset, interrupting his squawking. He fell blessedly silent while we all gaped at the fall and destruction of the two spaceships. I'd mostly ignored his chirping before and after.

I finish my summary with, "Commencing Phase Three."

Another quick subdue on the command hub, then I flick to a different menu. Taking a deep breath, I swipe the icon. The words 'Outgoing Call' fill the screen.

If Salam is lucky enough to be on one of the remaining four ships, does his own name appear as the caller on his new hub? Or maybe it's Tallai's name, depending on whose device I'm using now. Perhaps I'm registering as unknown since they've claimed other command hubs.

A click. The screen shows 'Connected.' Rasping breath husks from the device. I talk before he can open his beak.

"Surrender now and we might be merciful, though it's not what you deserve."

"Insolent, soft-fleshed, puny *human*," Salam hisses. "I will skin you alive myself until you are nothing but mewling and bloodied muscle."

Hunter tenses behind me. I pat his arm.

"How are you going to do that while you're cowering up there, hiding behind your weapons?" I say, striving to keep my voice calm. "Come down here and face what you've created."

Muffled snaps and buzzes drift from the speaker, as if someone is arguing in the background, but it's too indistinct for the translation tech in my ears to pick it up.

"Oh, and Salam?" I say sweetly. "Bring Tallai, too. Unless you're both fucking cowards."

I jab the disconnect button on furious spluttering.

That oughta do it.

"Christ, Maia," Greg says, "that grin on your face is menacing."

Ah, so that's why my cheeks ache. I massage my jaw. My heart knocks against my sternum, too fast and too hard. Adrenaline jitters through my fingers.

Steph scoops up her discarded riot shield, gouged but still whole. "What if they decide to cut their losses and vaporise us, our Protectorate included?"

"Then they win," I say softly.

"So we're banking everything on their hurt pride?"

"Well, having been through an apocalypse, an alien abduction, and now a space invasion, I think we can safely say nothing is certain." The grin, more a grimace, stretches my face again. "Except for the arrogance of Creators."

A tiny sparkle detaches from the base of the spaceship that contained the slime puddles. It shimmers towards us, zipping to a plateau on the east of our hill. The land becomes a ridge merging with the only other remaining peak of the eleven that formed the Pentland Hills. The position shelters them from the activity of the WAGS and angels on our northern slope, putting them out of their line of sight. Steph and Greg restore their riot shield barrier.

The shuttle entrance clunks open. A long, backward-jointed leg slinks from the shadows, encased in a tight bodysuit. A hunched chest and scaly wings emerge into the sunlight, everything dark and grey. Then a bright slash of violet. A beak of pointed teeth and a bony crest as tall as a shark's fin.

Salam'ack'tai'moran. Salam to his enemies.

Tallai stalks at his heels, shorter and lighter than the other Creator, but no less cruel or disdainful. A sheen of purple ripples on his wings.

It takes my brain three seconds of blinking to process the weirdness of Salam and Tallai standing on the grassy plateau of a hill, the shape of them a mish-mash of stork, vulture, and dinosaur. I'm also more used to seeing them surrounded by the aesthetics of their ancient civilisation—ferny spectator boxes

120

to witness the angels challenge and abuse each other, corridors of gleaming turquoise and pearl, the domed room of screens at the heart of their spaceship. Bronwyn prefers those trappings, too, and rarely ventures out these days.

Two more figures emerge from the shuttle's maw. They have humanoid bodies in some kind of mechanical suit and glass helmets full of fluid where slimy creatures stare at us from big, unblinking eyes.

The Creators of the blob warriors. As if there were any doubt.

They each have a command hub on their wrists, like Salam and Tallai. Nothing that looks like a weapon, though I wouldn't be surprised if the command hub has that functionality, too.

Not that I know what freaking setting it is. 'Protect', maybe?

Each Protectorate ship has a Creator crew of three, so that leaves one on the blob warriors' ship—the Creator in charge of the healing ward.

The walking slug tanks stand in a rough line with Salam and Tallai, though two steps back. Is it deference to the Creators in charge of the warrior angels or just so they can use them as shields if things go awry?

Let's hope it's the latter. Those smug bastards have enough ego. The last thing they need is a boost.

We survey each other across the short expanse of grass and scattered heath. Dev and Hunter nock their rifles to their shoulders in perfect synchrony, the barrels unwavering on their previous masters. Steady fingers curl around the triggers. Salam clicks his beak, then licks his teeth with a dry, leathery tongue as grey and pitted as his skin.

"I see you learned nothing from trying to stand against us," he says, raising the irritating buzz of his voice to account for the distance. "Your minor victory has made you complacent. But I will make you regret."

"The only regret I have is showing you mercy."

Salam's violet eyes settle on me instead of glaring at his creations. "Mercy is your weakness. One of many."

"I've learned that lesson now, but you still need to learn yours."

Salam chuckles, the sound like rocks cracking and grinding together. "What lesson could *you* teach *me?*"

"You should have left us alone." The words rush out, hot with the fear and pain of our shared history. "Our minor victory was only a prelude. You've brought *this* on yourself."

Tallai's wings flare, slapping the bubble head of the Creator standing closest to him. Salam cackles at my expense.

"Do you truly think to defeat us with my own faction? You will choke on your conceit. You are outnumbered and outmatched, even with our stolen property. It is *you* who should surrender."

I'm squeezing the butt of the Glock at my hip, my knuckles bunching rhythmic and white, and force myself to stop.

"You've sicced two of your factions on us, yet we're not defeated."

Salam narrows the bright slash of his eyes. "What have you done with my warriors, insolent human?"

One of the slimy things rolls in its bubble helmet. Displeasure? Agreement? Or maybe it was stretching.

I force a smile on my numb lips, my skin chilled despite the summer heat. "I'm making them *my* warriors."

The flap of wings signals the arrival of angels. A contingent of them hovers in the sky between us and the Creators. Their rifles mirror the aim of Hunter and Dev.

Salam flicks them a glance, then bares his teeth. "I have had my fill of your arrogance."

Before I can splutter at his glaring hypocrisy, he swipes a quadruple-jointed finger on his command hub. I tense, expecting the blue flash of another soulreaving laser gun or maybe something that will control my angels despite their lack of cybernetics.

The Creators like to brag about their technology, but won't share it with anyone they consider less advanced. Which is probably ninety-nine percent of the worlds they've encountered.

Steph and Greg brace their shoulders against their shields. Dev and Hunter tense, staring down the sights of their guns. My fingers twitch over the screen of the command hub on my left wrist, my arm across my stomach to keep the movement as unobtrusive as possible.

Not that I have any clue how to counteract a hub weapon or other aggressive command beyond 'subdue'. Maybe that's what 'protect' is for. Or 'shelter'. It could even be 'sleep'. I don't bloody know.

The sky fills with twinkling reflections.

"Ah, fuck, man," Greg sighs. "Here we go again."

Every shuttle from the three remaining Protectorate ships streaks towards our crowded hill.

The Creators may be arrogant, but they're not foolish.

Dammit.

18

"All remaining Protectorate factions now incoming," I bark into my mic. Curran probably won't appreciate it, since he's the one who likes to do the barking around here.

"Acknowledged," he barks back, sounding disgruntled. "Ground support—prepare to defend. Air support, commence Phase Four."

I drop my gaze from the descending shuttles to Salam and Tallai. They can't smirk with their rigid beaks, but their satisfaction sizzles across the space between us. I suck in a long breath, then ease it out. Thirty thousand warriors zip closer. Who knows what kind of Frankenstein creatures they'll be.

"Shoot to wound," I say.

Dev and Hunter's KS-1 rifles kick in tandem. My heart kicks with them.

But nothing happens. No splash of silver blood. No shriek of pain. No crumpled and writhing Creators regretting their life choices.

Hunter grits his teeth. "There is some kind of shield. The bullets stick and then fall into the grass."

I didn't see the fate of the bullets, the movement too quick for my simple human eyeballs, but something ripples, orange and cobalt, in a dome shape around the Creators. Salam's eyes widen before he schools his expression to evil vulture. Tallai's wings twitch. The slug tanks ease further behind the other two Creators.

Perhaps they thought the angels wouldn't shoot at them, even without the cybernetics. They've had years of following the Creators' command. Treating them like gods. Maybe they thought some behaviour would be ingrained. Somewhat misguided, since Uziyah manhandled Salam during our spaceship encounter and showed no lingering deference to his Creators once he was on our side. We weren't trying to kill them then, and I don't want to kill them now.

Though that may not be up to me.

Greg's geeky grin manages a weak splutter. "A force field? Are you shitting me?"

Hunter slides him a look. "I am not *shitting* you."

The shuttles zoom to the nineteen empty vessels already ranged across the base of the hill. They hover above them to create stacks of two, the remaining shuttles pairing off to leave one bobbing alone. Entrances clunk open and warriors spill out.

"What the fuck am I looking at?" Steph grumbles.

"*Now* we're in *Star Wars*," Greg says.

It's too much for my brain to process at once. Instead, I get snapshots—feathered wings and a maroon, segmented body; grey skin and a bulbous head with big, black eyes; a green, four-armed Minotaur. The different factions remain in their units and swarm up the hill, the density of their numbers obscuring the grass and heath and gorse beneath their churning feet. The ground rumbles under my boots.

"I bet it's no coincidence that people described those grey

guys when they claimed to have been abducted by aliens," Steph says.

Greg jiggles behind his shield, excitement creeping into his voice. "I bet they were monitoring us. Abduct a few specimens and stick a probe up their arse to see if humanity is behaving."

"I bet—"

"This isn't the time to speculate," I say over Steph. "We have to disable that force field and capture the Creators. If we have them, we might get the rest to surrender."

Steph slaps Greg's arm. "Goddammit, you dragged me into your sci-fi babble."

"Sorry, Maia." Greg pouts at Steph and rubs his arm.

"I will try," Hunter says. "Dev—watch my back and guard our humans."

Dev gives a curt nod, his stare unwavering down the scope of his KS-1. A curl of blond hair sticks to his cheekbone. Hunter drops his rifle on its sling and pulls an iron sword from goodness knows where. Black wings flare wide. He launches from the peak of our hill and swoops towards the Creators' protected huddle.

Rifle fire drags my gaze to the slope. The silent Protectorate clash with the warrior angels and WAGS.

It seems the mutant panthers were the only faction to shriek their intent and vicious glee.

I bend to my command hub. Highlight—tap—subdue. The flying centipedes go rigid and drop from their tangle with the angels. Six humanoid arms and six centipede legs pedal at the air as they fall. The grey aliens fold their long-limbed bodies in half, as if their giant skulls have suddenly become too heavy to hold upright. Membranous frills shiver on the heads of the green Minotaurs as they crumple to all four knees.

"You cannot fight us," Salam shouts above the thud of bodies and the excited yells of the WAGS. "Your persistence will only amplify our wrath."

I have to give him credit—his voice doesn't wobble one bit as Hunter reaches the force field and stabs his sword at it. An orange and cobalt crackle flings him backwards in a ruffle of feathers and tattered clothes. He slams on his back, his iron blade broken in half.

"Hunter!" I gasp.

Hunter flips himself onto his feet. Tallai and the two slug tanks swipe at their command hubs. Salam glares at Hunter, his arm held out in front so the screen of his device points at his own sunken chest. Hunter tosses his ruined sword aside and stalks towards them. Bursts from Dev's rifle stop a couple of green Minotaurs. They collapse into the grass, legs pedalling and scouring the dirt. Their furred hooves are concave underneath, rather than solid or fleshy.

Screams and gunfire echo across the hill. Blue streaks decorate the sky and sizzle into the heather.

Hunter returns Salam's glare, halting where the force field must be, though it's invisible when nothing is hitting it.

"The grey aliens have laser guns," Steph says, her expression grim as she watches the chaos through the blur of her shield.

Greg's mouth turns down. "The winged bug things have throwing stars. And they don't have a face, man. It's fucking creepy."

I subdue the Protectorate. Again. And again, wrestling for control with Tallai and the other two Creators. Salam's hub must be the one maintaining the force field.

Hunter places his palm against air. The force field ripples, but doesn't zap him back. He leans his weight against it. Salam flaps his beak, the words lost in the cacophony of human panic, gunfire, and the stamp of thousands and thousands of feet.

My subdue commands last minutes.

Then seconds.

A flying centipede scuttles to its spiked legs and shakes its head, the smooth maroon skin unmarked by anything resembling eyes, a nose, or a mouth. Glowing blue throwing stars appear in its three-fingered hands, one for each of its six arms. With a deft flick, the warrior whips the soulreavers in a blue blur across the battlefield. One embeds itself in a WAGS' armpit. Her scream is swallowed by the fight. Dust puffs beneath stampeding feet. The throwing star whizzes back to the waiting hand of the warrior, as if magnetised.

I tap my hub. Tap, tap, *tap*. My jaw aches from gritting my teeth.

The Creators must not have realised I was subduing their first wave of warriors using the command hub. Why else would it have been so easy, when it's now impossible?

Hunter rams his shoulder into the force field, then his fists. He lands a bone-shuddering kick that would've separated a human's head from their shoulders, but does nothing to the force field except for the taunting flicker of colour that reveals its domed extent.

"They're cancelling my commands as soon as I make them," I say, my voice high. "And Hunter isn't having any luck."

Throwing stars clatter into our shields. The three of us yelp and duck, though Steph and Greg were already crouched. Dev's rifle barks. An empty magazine bounces off his boot, and he slots another.

"I have one magazine left," he says, not taking his eyes from his targets.

Hunter thuds next to me, tucking his wings tight to his back. "I can touch the force field without injury, but not penetrate it. Any weapon elicits an electric shock."

I relay our issues to Curran, abandoning my ineffective subdue commands to the overwhelming might of the Creators. Grey aliens prowl up the slope, firing steady streaks of blue from cream-coloured guns. WAGS cower behind shields and vehicles. Dust turns to paste in the sweat on my arms and clogs the air with the taste of ozone. Angels wrestle flying centipedes. Iron bullets smack into skulls.

But it's not enough.

If Salam can form a force field via his command hub, then I can, too. It won't give us an advantage, but it might allow me enough time to come up with something. Anything to halt the wall of warriors rushing towards us.

Salam's tyranny will triumph over my dead body.

"Oh, Jesus," Greg groans.

I follow his line of sight to a clump of green Minotaurs. Fear cramps my gut and pebbles my skin in a wash of ice.

A Minotaur hoof kicks out and attaches to a WAGS' face. Sickly blue borders the obscene contact. The soldier jerks. Powder sifts to the ground around his crumpled clothes. The Minotaur rears. Its fore-hooves sucker onto two more soldiers. Before they're even dusted, the creature reaches for another two soldiers, grabbing their uniforms in its fists and hoisting them off the ground, their legs kicking. Yellow froth bubbles from the Minotaur's bared torso and horse parts. The warrior ignores the wounds and palms the terrified faces of the soldiers with its remaining two hands. Except it doesn't have hands on its last two limbs, but more soulreaving suckers. The creature is briefly obscured by a billow of dust before it leaps clear and thunders up the hill surrounded by its brethren.

"They're almost on us, Maia," Steph bleats.

I scrabble at the command hub. Sweat pools beneath my body armour and shredded t-shirt. I jab the protect command and hurt my fingertip, my skin blanching white.

Nothing happens.

The weight of the advancing Protectorate feels like it will flatten our peak to a nub to join the rest of the mangled Pentland Hills. They'll steamroll right over us and slaughter the rest of the world just as easily.

The warriors are twenty metres away, and climbing.

Ten.

I swipe the screen. Swipe, swipe, swipe. At 'sleep', the factions slow their sprint to a trot. Anything with eyeballs blinks and looks around. Limbs hesitate, held aloft and ready to gallop. The hesitation lasts five long heartbeats.

Feet, suckers, and insect legs pound and pierce the solid dirt. Lasers sizzle and flash. Throwing stars whirr and clatter into shields. Our rifle fire splutters and dwindles.

Eight metres away.

Seven.

Where the hell is our air support? We're all about to be dust.

I pray, and hit the shelter icon.

19

Grey aliens level their laser guns. Flying centipedes whoosh over them, throwing stars poised. Green Minotaurs bunch their haunches, and leap. Glowing blue sucker hooves aim for Greg's face. Dev reaches for him, his fingers extended, his expression panicked. Steph screams.

Flesh and chitin thuds into an invisible barrier. An orange and cobalt dome flares around us, covering me and Hunter, and Steph, Greg, and Dev, with a metre of space beyond our huddled group. Throwing stars spark and rebound, sinking into the exposed Protectorate. Bones snap as bodies pile on bodies and form a living wall against our dome. Suckers flex on the force field, the cavity filled with an eerie, sickening blue.

"I should've tried 'shelter' first," I mutter.

I was given a stern warning by the scientists when they handed over the command hub—no playing around with the functions. But I really could have done with the practise.

A shaking hand grips my forearm where I'm holding it in front of my chest, mirroring Salam with his force field, though his position is obscured by the crush of warriors smashing on our barrier. Shadows swallow the sun and turn the inside of our bubble to twilight. I follow the hand to Steph's pale face and huge eyes. She's engulfed in muscled arms and sapphire wings, smooshed next to Greg in Dev's hold. The riot shields lie on the crushed vegetation at their feet.

"You're doing amazing, Maia," she gasps. "Don't let those fuckers make you doubt yourself. You're better than them. You can win this."

The smack of flesh on force field slows to nothing. A small square of blue sky remains at the apex of our dome, the shaft of sunlight bathing Hunter and bringing out the violet and green shimmer in his wings. Beauty surrounded by carnage. The sudden quiet sends shivers down my spine.

Have they dusted all the WAGS? Are my warrior angels out of ammo? Who's protecting them while I hide in a bubble?

I coax my lips into a quivering smile. "I think you might be biased, Steph."

"I've seen it. You stopped the apocalypse. You saved us on the spaceship. *All* of us." She scans our claustrophobic dome and the alien bodies pressed against it. "You'll save us now."

"Not all of us," I whisper, tears clogging my throat. "I don't know what I'm doing."

"Doesn't matter. You'll figure it out."

"How can you have such faith in me?"

"You're my best friend."

Dev relinquishes his grip on his beloved. Two steps, and we collide in the middle, my face smothered in her boobs. I inhale Parma Violets and jasmine, the scent blunting the spikes of my anxiety. Greg cuddles in from behind, and I take a moment just to *breathe*.

An increasing roar pries us apart. A steady *thwup-thwup-thwup* shudders into our dome. Our shaft of sunlight widens as the bodies of the Protectorate peel away.

Salam and Tallai sneer from behind the protection of their

force field while the attention of the two slug tanks remains on the sky. A squadron of fighter jets blasts over our hill and streaks for the four hulking spaceships loitering above us.

The vessels are empty of warriors, but three of them still have their full contingent of three Creators, with one medical Creator left on the slime puddle ship where Salam and Tallai hitched a ride.

Rockets disengage from the underside of the jets in a plume of smoke and fire. Helicopters bank across the hillside and hover into a neat line above the empty shuttles. The lateral doors of the passenger compartments slide open and gun barrels bristle out. Rifles bark, spitting empty casings into the heath and gorse and bouncing off the shuttles with a musical ping.

"Buckthorn!" Curran snaps in my ear. "Reform your defensive position. Haile is bringing reinforcements and ammo."

Rockets detonate harmlessly on the spaceships' shields, a flicker of orange and cobalt sheltering them in a massive bubble. Golden beams flare from somewhere in the darkness of angles and lines. Roaring jets explode and fireball to the ground.

Looks like Reynold learned nothing from the destruction of his space squadron. I told him not to attack the ships. It seems the only way to get around their automated shields and defences is to copy Abayankari.

All our stolen, retrofitted shuttles have been blown to smithereens, but we have plenty of vessels to choose from ranged at the bottom of the hill. I doubt anyone would volunteer to be a kamikaze pilot, though.

"It has reformed," I yell at Curran. "They're overwhelmed."

A maelstrom of fighting covers the slope below us. Markian swings his iron sword, deflecting laser fire, and buries the tip

WE ARE NOT CONQUERED

in the unblinking black eye of a grey alien. His dagger punches under the chin of a Minotaur. Frothing Protectorate blanket the ground.

But, again, it's not enough.

A soldier drops from an open helicopter compartment, their uniform stippled with throwing stars. Their body dissolves to a plume of dust and their clothes flutter to the grass. Flying centipedes converge on the helicopters. Tornadoes of dust swirl beneath screaming rotor blades. One by one, the helicopters tip sideways and crunch into the dirt, less spectacularly than the fall of the spaceships. Explosions rumble under my boots. The shriek of retreating jets, the zap of lasers, and the grunts of struggling warriors fill the vacuum of the rotor noise.

Markian fights in a circle of sweeping wings and whirling blades. A ruby feather puffs into the air. A Minotaur rears behind him. Sucker hooves slam into his shoulders and drive him to his knees. Two more suckers slap to the sides of his face and hold his head steady. His wings droop. A grey alien approaches the pinioned, nauseated angel with an object clasped in their long-fingered hands.

"No!" I gasp.

My gaze flies to Salam. Triumph blazes in his violet eyes.

The collar clamps around Markian's throat. The band glows a sickly green, forming bright lines and dots through the sheen of metal. My angel stops fighting. Suckers retract from his flesh. Markian stands smoothly, grabs another angel by the neck, and punches him in the face.

"Those fucking collars, man," Greg says.

"No," I whisper, and keep whispering it.

I try to subdue the warriors using my spare command hub.

134

They waver for a millisecond before the order is cancelled. The three Protectorate factions work together to overpower the angels and collar them, the cybernetics turning them into the obedient and violent robots I hate. Mindless Creator tools.

This can't be happening again.

Panic claws at my gut. The thought of a collared Hunter, cold and cruel and wanting only to please his masters, has my knees wobbling. My eyes dart around the heaving battlefield, looking for something—*anything*—that will stop this.

I have to stop this.

"There are Protectorate heading for Edinburgh," Curran says, anxiety blunting his usual bark. "Buckthorn—"

"Stupid, deluded human," Salam calls gleefully while I try not to vomit. "Your hope is a weakness. And one I enjoy crushing."

I spin away from him, breathless and unsteady, a desperate plan half-forming in my brain. "Dev, can you leave the force field?"

Without any hesitation, Dev sticks his arm out the edge of our barrier, invisible now since no one is attacking it.

"It tingles, but does not hurt," he says.

"Get Steph and Greg away from here. Hunter, too."

"Maia, what—"

I'm sprinting before Steph has finished her yelp of protest. I throw myself from the peak of our hill. My rifle bashes my hip. My boots thud on the packed ground, not quite as loud as my heartbeat. I hook the headset from my face to silence Curran's bleating and avoid the device melting my brain should my plan... spark something.

If this doesn't work, we're all dead. Humanity will become extinct under the wrath of the Creators and my angels will be reduced to slaves, forced once more to abuse each other, punish wayward civilisations, and service their Creators. And nothing more. No comforts, no affection. Just a harsh and bitter existence until they die from it.

Strong arms scoop me into a firm chest. My boots leave the ground, paddling at the air as I attempt to run. Black feathers flicker at the edges of my vision.

"Hunter, no! I need to—"

"I see what you are doing." His words rumble against my back, his warm breath in my ear. "And I am coming with you."

"But it might do nothing. Or kill us both."

His soft lips graze my cheekbone. "Then we go together."

His wings catch the air and he swoops for the plateau. Salam drags his smug gaze from the splendour of his victory to Hunter stooping for him, me cuddled in his arms. I keep my forearm held out in front, the force field stable despite the rapid movement.

Or the command hub seems fine with it, anyway.

Salam's eyes widen. He squawks something. The attention of Tallai and the two slug tanks snaps to us. Salam stabs a multi-jointed finger at the screen of his command hub.

Time slows. Grass bends beneath the brush of the force field. The slug tanks turn, as if to run. Tallai clamps a spindly hand on their shoulders.

Orange and cobalt ripples at the contact point of our force fields. The domes spark and pop and flash a blinding white. A weight punches into my middle, flinging me backwards. I land on hard muscles and velvet feathers. Everything crackles—my ears, the sky, the fillings in my teeth.

Are my eyes open or closed? Am I breathing? Is *Hunter* breathing?

All I can feel is a burning in my wrist. All I can hear is the stutter-stop-start of my heartbeat.

And Hunter, frantic, as he calls my name.

20

My wrist is on fire. A sharp rip of pain tugs a groan from me, then blessed coolness. The ringing in my ears fades to words.

"Open your eyes, Maia," Hunter says.

I open my eyes.

Black wings eclipse the sun. Smoke curls from the feathers. My smouldering angel. Tender hands cup my face and equally tender lips find mine. I'm engulfed by warmth and the scent of ice.

"Are you okay?" Hunter whispers against my mouth.

"I... I think so?" I croak.

His sigh brushes my jaw and stirs my hair. Stiff heather branches poke my neck and scalp. Hunter sits on his haunches and tucks his wings away. I squint against the sunlight. Three silhouettes crowd close.

"My wrist hurts," I say. "What happened?"

"You saved us." Greg kneels at my side, carefully wrapping a bandage around my forearm.

"You also burned the shit out of your wrist," Steph says, standing over me, Dev's arm around her waist. "You'll need Bronwyn's healing tank. The wound was deep. At least second degree."

Greg swallows thickly, a hint of green washing over his

cheekbones. "Don't remind me. I had to look at it before I put the dressing on."

"We cut the hub off in case it affected your circulation." Steph nods at the grass.

I turn my head, losing a strand of hair to the grasping heather. Cracks fissure across the screen of the command hub, the shape of the device distorted. The sliced strap has more of my skin on it than I'd like.

Greg's throat clicks. "Stop talking about it, man, unless you want me to barf."

"You're a bit queasy for a medic, prickles," Steph smirks.

Dev squeezes her waist. "Our prickly pear is a gentle soul."

Greg huffs and rolls his eyes, pinning my dressing in place. He straightens and slots himself into Dev's other side, Dev's arm sliding around his hips. Hunter helps me to my feet and holds my elbow when I sway.

"Are *you* okay?" I peer up at him through a fizz of dizziness that settles after a minute. Smoke continues to waft from his feathers and the singed hems of his black top. The gaping and bloodless wounds from the mutant panther claws are already starting to knit together and shrink in size.

His lips curve. "Scorched, but no lasting damage."

"So, it worked?"

"See for yourself."

He pivots out of my way, keeping a steady hand on my uninjured arm. I prod the second command hub, and the screen brightens. Still working.

"Nice to have you back on your feet, Buckthorn."

I lift my head to find the voice, my brain a bit fuzzy. Haile holds her KS-1 rifle in two hands, the barrel pointed at four figures hunched on the ground. Her cap perches at a jaunty angle on her greying auburn hair, the rest of her khaki uniform immaculate. My t-shirt is torn and covered in dried froth. I blink, and my sluggish mind fills in the details of the creatures at her feet.

Salam shows his teeth. He's sitting on his backwards-jointed knees next to Tallai. Scratches on his arms ooze silver through his ripped bodysuit. Zip-ties bind their knobbly wrists and ankles together, though Salam's right wrist is a weeping mess of blackened skin, melted bodysuit, and grey tissue.

Is that what mine looks like?

My turn to swallow hard.

"He let us remove the hub since it was eating into his bony arm, but he's been reluctant for us to dress the wound," Haile says.

A mangled command hub sits in the grass next to three that appear undamaged. Tallai's wrist is bare, as are the slug tanks', apart from the zip-ties. The other two Creators hug the bent knees of their mechanical suits. One shifts on its butt with a glug from the tank of liquid that serves as its head. Unblinking eyes flick between me and Haile.

"I do not need your primitive medicine," Salam hisses, "you insolent hu—"

Haile's rifle barrel raps him between the nostrils. "Shut your beak."

I knew I liked her.

Salam snaps his mouth closed, his long fingers bunching into fists. Tallai ruffles his scaly wings, but stays silent. Violet eyes glare at me.

Bronwyn has been quite liberal with the translation fluid, dosing anyone who wanted it—military and world leaders, scientists, curious members of the public. The stuff self-replicates, so it never runs out.

"Where are my angels?" I say to Haile. "Where's the rest of your brigade?"

My eyes follow her nod to the slope of the hill, as if I can't notice the details until they're pointed out to me.

The shock of the force field collision has really messed with my head. I feel a bit spaced out.

Soldiers swarm over the slope. Limp aliens, centipedes, and Minotaurs are loaded into troop carriers and spirited away. Clumps of angels hold struggling figures on the ground. Columns of smoke billow from crashed helicopters and the crater of the fallen spaceships. Sirens wail.

"You, Hunter, and the Fantastic Four were knocked out for a minute after you ran into their force field," Steph says, surveying the hive of activity. "All the Protectorate with cybernetics also collapsed, and they're still unconscious. About a third of the angels were collared. The rest are holding them down."

"I want to see, but... uh, I don't think my legs are working yet."

Hunter lifts me into a bridal carry, my shoulder against his chest, my knees bent over his arm. The world swirls before it behaves itself.

I glance from Steph to Haile and the bound Creators. "Would you watch them with Haile?"

Steph smirks. "Sure thing, Boss. Go check on your angels. These sneaky bastards won't be slipping any bonds this time."

Hunter picks his way down the slope, his view obscured by my body in his arms. I tilt the screen of my remaining hub, then highlight and subdue every cybernetically enhanced organism on the hill, careful not to twist my bandaged wrist. Nothing cancels my command, and I raise my gaze to the sky.

"Has there been any movement from the spaceships?"

Hunter shakes his head. "They will watch and wait. We have the advantage."

"Is it really over?"

"Almost."

My fingertips sneak through the rents in his shirt to stroke warm and silky skin. A slow smile tugs at his mouth, but he says nothing more. We reach the closest clump of angels.

Markian thrashes against the hands pinning him. His splayed wings look like sprays of bright arterial blood. At Hunter's approach, he quits struggling and glares through a mass of curly, brown hair.

"Release me and heed your Creators," he growls in a low and menacing voice, "or you will be punished."

The collar at his throat paints a sickly green glow on his skin. He continues to spout slavish nonsense about obeying their masters and blah blah blah. I scan the four golden-winged angels subduing him the old-fashioned way.

"Can you rip the collar off without hurting him or yourself?"

A wordless glance passes between the warriors. A male with eyes as golden as his wings clamps Markian's arm between his knees and runs his fingers around the band. His biceps flex. The collar crunches and fizzes, then breaks in two. The green lights stutter and die. The angel drops the pieces to the dusty ground. We all stare at Markian.

"How do you feel?" I say.

Markian blinks. Tension eases from his face and relaxes his scowl.

"I feel... like myself again."

The angel who removed Markian's collar holds out a hand

and pulls him to his feet. Markian blinks a few more times and looks at the carnage of dust and unconscious Protectorate.

"We won the battle? What happened?"

Hunter's arms cuddle me closer.

"Maia," he says, his voice full of pride.

My cheeks flush.

I like the praise, but I don't deserve it. All I've done is flap around and get people killed. I have no idea what I'm doing ninety percent of the time. It works out by pure luck, not skill.

Though I can pretend to be leadery for a little longer.

"Destroy the collars," I say. "Crush them into little bits."

Markian and the four other angels scatter to spread the word and assist their brethren in freeing the rest.

Removing the collar and ending its evil influence was how I'd hoped to rescue Hunter when he was collared on the spaceship, but I didn't have the strength of angels and waited too long. The cybernetics grew in his brain like a tumour.

Hunter nuzzles my ear. "Do you wish to return to the yappy human and your best friend?"

"Yes, please."

His black wings flare and launch us into the sky, flapping for the peak of our hill that juts out of the sea of chaos like an iceberg. He lands, and lowers my boots to a patch of grass.

"Your commanding officer is trying to get your attention," he says before I can do more than return Steph's smile of greeting. The words 'commanding officer' use the same tone as if he'd said 'trifling annoyance'.

When I blink at him, Hunter jerks his chin at the headset dangling from my collar. I slot it back into my ear.

I think I need a lie down.

"Hello?"

"Buckthorn! For Christ—" Curran sucks a long breath of air in and out. I picture him pinching the bridge of his nose. "Status report," he barks.

I rub a fingertip to the tension headache gathering beneath my left eyebrow. "I destroyed the force field protecting the Creators by ramming mine into it. We have four prisoners—"

"Haile has already relayed this information, which you would know if you'd been listening to your comms."

"I was a bit busy getting my brain and my wrist fried."

"Buckthorn has been injured in the altercation, sir," Haile chips in, her words repeating in my ear after a second's lag.

"And now I'm about to start Phase Five—question the prisoners and communicate with the spaceships."

"There was no Phase Five," Curran says.

"Yeah, it's a surprise to me, too."

"I had no doubts," Steph says, her gaze and her gun on Salam, Tallai, and the slug tanks.

Greg holds up his finger and thumb with a small gap between. "Mine were tiny. Minuscule. Not even worth mentioning."

"I knew we would win." Dev and Hunter share a smug grin.

"Bring the prisoners to the facility for questioning," Curran says. "Haile—stay and oversee the Protectorate extraction. Do we need to worry about them waking up?"

Haile, her gun aim steady on Salam's surly beak, scoops a device from the ground. "I have a spare command hub. Buckthorn can show me how to use it."

A hiss shivers out of Tallai. From his cramped position, he's all elbows and knees and bristling wings.

Salam cackles. "You think you have won? Look to the sky, ignorant humans. We have four spaceships awaiting our command. They will witness and judge your actions, and deliver the punishment you deserve."

"Greg," Steph says, "get your sock."

Salam sneers at her. "You may bind and gag us as before, but your savage race will see its own end."

"Why did you come with them?" I say to the silent slug tanks.

The slimy creatures twist to look at each other without moving their humanoid bodies.

"Do not talk to them," Salam splutters. "*I* am the authority here."

"Answer me truthfully and you'll receive fair treatment."

Salam scoffs. "She lies. Human morality forbids the abuse of prisoners of war."

I meet Salam's bright, slashing eyes. His haughty expression fades at whatever he sees on my face.

"Not all of us are human," I say softly.

21

"Why did you come with them?"

The slugs roll in their globular heads to regard each other, like they did when I first asked the question over an hour ago. Liquid slops, their tanks not entirely full to the brim. Handcuffs bind their wrists to a metal bar in the centre of the table separating us.

The calm hush of air conditioning and the weight of tonnes of earth above our heads replace the chaos of the hill. Curran shifts next to me, the chair creaking under his blocky frame. I clasp my hands on the immaculate tabletop. Flecks of dried blood and dust float down. The command hub around my wrist clunks on the surface. The bandage is gone from my other arm, the skin of my hand and wrist sparkling and clean. Hunter stands, intense and immovable, at my back.

He whisked me to Bronwyn and her tank of pink goo. He's always tried not to hurt me, but ever since he was forced to on the spaceship, any injury to me, no matter how small, causes him distress. I was still a bit dizzy to argue or recoil at the surroundings of the Protectorate ship and the awful familiarity of the healing ward.

"Salam and Tallai can't hear you," I say to the slug tanks' silence. "They're not in control anymore."

The other two Creators are in an identical room neighbouring ours—cuffed to the table, monitored through one-way glass, a single door of thick steel.

Curran wanted to question them first, but I convinced him to let them stew. They'll be fuming at being ignored in favour of the slug tanks. I made sure they saw us entering the room with them, while they were led to another.

Petty? Maybe, but immensely satisfying, especially when Salam's indignant squawk echoed down the corridor.

"They lead our province. They demand and we follow."

The translated words overlie the bubbling vibration of the slug tank's original language. They have no visible mouth to talk from, though they have gills running the length of their slimy bodies. Pink spots speckle the head of the Creator who spoke, beneath six tiny, fringed antennae. The second creature has yellow spots and four antennae.

Curran jerks forward. "And who leads *them?* Will they come to their aid? Will the Creators in the other ships attack us?"

Well, he lasted two seconds before butting in. That must have been torture for him.

The slug tanks share a glance. Their antennae flutter and cause ripples of liquid, but my translation fluid doesn't pick up any words. Maybe they can communicate telepathically, or they've worked together for so long, they can read body language.

"Did you want to come?" I slide a look at the fidgeting Curran.

Must not shush him in front of the aliens.

"It is not our place to want," Pink-spots says.

"You sound like the Protectorate."

That causes a roll of agitation. Or a roll of something. It's not easy to extrapolate the actions of a slug.

"What are your names?"

Back to simple questions. I need them to relax if they're going to talk.

Sound vibrates through their liquid heads, but barely translates into something recognisable. I pick out the only parts I understand.

"Would you be offended if I called you Pat and Dot?"

The slug tanks twist their whole bodies to look at each other this time. Curran tuts, but I ignore him.

"That would be acceptable," Pat of the pink spots says.

A bubble drifts to the surface of Dot's tank and pops lightly. "We are not so sensitive."

Ooh, was that a dig at Salam and Tallai? Interesting...

"And do you want to be referred to as he, she, or they?"

"They," the slug tanks say together. "Gender is irrelevant on our planet," Pat continues.

Greg would be geeking out right now, interrupting with a million science and biology questions. He stayed behind on the hill with Steph and Dev to help Haile supervise the clean up. They were erecting floodlights when we left, the sun somehow dipping towards the horizon already.

Time flies when you're battling to save the world.

Still no word or movement from the other spaceships, even when we dragged the four Creators away to the Roslin Institute.

I hope it's a good sign. I'm too tired and sore to fight anymore.

"Are you hungry? Can we get you anything to eat or drink?"

"Buckthorn..." Curran hisses under his breath.

Honestly, how did he climb so high in the military if he's this impatient? I understand his urgency—the other Creators could attack at any moment, they could be summoning help—but I promised the slug tanks fair treatment if they spoke the truth, and that's what they'll get.

Hunter growls, short and sharp. Curran crosses his arms and sinks in his chair.

He argued with me for ten minutes about letting me lead the questioning of the Creators. But I command the angels, and in their eyes, that means I'm superior.

Or probably not, since I'm human and I stole them, but I thought it was worth a shot.

"Our suits sustain us," Pat says, "though we thank you for your hospitality. It would also not offend us if you needed to procure your own sustenance."

I give them a nod of acknowledgement, and Pat bobs in their tank to return it.

I stuffed a protein bar in my gob ten minutes ago, though I didn't want it. My stomach is full of stress and dread of the unknown. Maybe I'll feel hungry again when I'm not so exhausted.

"Salam and Tallai are the liars," I say. "The tyrants. If I promise to do something, I'll do it. And I'm not very good with authority."

Curran manages to turn his snort into a cough. Hunter's feathers whisper behind us, and Curran's shoulders twitch.

"They would be displeased at your butchering of their names," Pat says.

A smirk tugs at my mouth. "Why do you think I do it?"

Dot gurgles, earning an unblinking-eyed glare from Pat. Dot writhes in their tank and stares at the table.

Dot seems to be the younger of the two. Higher energy. Perhaps they grow more antennae as they get older, similar to the height of the bony crest indicating age in Salam and Tallai's species.

I lean closer, sliding my elbows on the table. "So, to return to my original question—why did you come with them?"

"Coercion," Pat says.

My heart skips. Now we're getting somewhere.

"Are the other Creators with you in the same position?"

"Not the creators of the foforolona. They are like-minded. To subjugate is to be all-powerful. If you are not a master, you are a slave."

"Which Protectorate are the foforolona?"

Dot lifts their arms, the cuff on their wrist scraping along the bar and preventing full movement. They curl their fingers into claws and make a yipping noise.

The mutant panthers. Abayankari's bloody revenge removed that problem for us, though I wish she hadn't sacrificed herself.

Uziyah wouldn't have wanted that.

I rub my chest at the kick of pain.

The sight of him laid out on a slab in the healing ward—so big, so strong, yet conquered by death—had the tears welling, and I forced myself away.

We'll honour him properly soon. Him and Abayankari, though her remains have drifted to the stars.

Hunter's warm palm cups my shoulder, and I realise I've been quiet too long.

"What about the four spaceships that stayed in your universe—why didn't they come?"

Pat wriggles in their tank. "They are bolder. Their civilisations are more independent. We rely heavily on the shirivaks for trade."

"The shirivaks?"

"The species name of... the ones you call Salam and Tallai."

Dot gives a bubbly giggle. "Salam and Tallai!"

They settle at a stern eyeball from Pat.

"Will the Creators in the ships above us be open to discussion?"

"It depends on what you are doing with our Protectorate," Pat says.

"We're removing their cybernetics and giving them free will."

Pat deflates into a slug pancake, their antennae drooping. Dot bobs in their tank.

"We have laboured under this heavy yoke for too long," Pat says on a bubbling sigh. "Striving for dominance. For perfection, when all life is perfectly imperfect. I am weary of the cruelty. I care not for the glory of my province."

Dot's eyes bug wider, threatening to pop from their slimy sockets. Their body twists in their tank.

Pat's been keeping secrets.

"I want to go home," Dot says.

Pat nods. "As do I."

I stand, probably a bit too abruptly given the screech of my chair and the flinch from Pat and Dot, who splodge against the rear of their tanks. Hunter's hand stays on my shoulder.

"I promise that if you truly want to be peaceful with us, then we'll let you go home." I pivot to Curran. "Remove their cuffs."

Curran splutters. "There is everything at stake here. We can't just—"

"I'm not saying let them roam free yet, but let them be comfortable while we talk to Salam and Tallai." I turn back to Pat and Dot while Curran grinds his jaw. "Is there anything else I can get you?"

Pat and Dot bend their mechanical suits in a low bow over

the table.

"You have given us more than we deserve," Pat says.

Curran, reluctantly, unlocks their handcuffs. Pat and Dot relax into their seats unlike a human, who would have immediately rubbed their wrists, whether the cuffs hurt them or not.

I slap Curran on the back on our way out the door. "Don't worry, Lieutenant General. You can lead now. Because this conversation is not going to be as pleasant."

22

Salam and Tallai, true to form, treat Curran's questions with disdain, offering nothing except for their absolute contempt of the human race. They threaten and demand and show no fear or remorse.

They are the fucking worst.

I had a mild panic attack before we entered their room—locked ribs, frozen limbs, throbbing pulse. Hunter cuddled me into the safety of his arms and told me I didn't have to go in. I didn't have to talk to them. He would attend to spare me the awfulness of their presence.

But I refuse to give those bastard vultures any opportunity to gloat. And I haven't forgotten Hunter's promise.

I'm not sure how I feel about it. I would be quite happy for them to rot away the rest of their miserable lives in a prison somewhere. No power, no respect. I want them to *break* at the shame and degradation of how far they've fallen. I want everyone to witness. I want—

Velvet black feathers brush my bare arms. My muscles ache from tension, a migraine thudding between my temples. I force my hands to unclench from their fists, and blood rushes to the pale indentation of my fingernails in my palms. I uncurl my spine and raise my gaze from my lap.

Salam sneers at me amidst Tallai's latest tirade. Not that I've been listening. We've been going round in circles for hours, excluding one short bathroom and tea break. Pat and Dot were content in their room, marvelling over the pack of cards I gave them to keep them occupied. Last I saw, they were bickering and building a pyramid.

Steph, Greg, and Dev have returned from the battleground, swapping with a fresh shift of WAGS who'll collect the last of the subdued Protectorate. They're waiting for me in the corridor for when this ordeal is finally done. Who knows when that'll be, since it's already gone midnight, and Salam and Tallai seem to gain energy from berating our inadequacies.

Midnight. I feel every second of this unending day in my bones.

Curran huffs for the thousandth time since we entered the room. "They're like you—they don't listen."

"I listen," I say, a spark of ire fuelling my weary body. "Mostly."

Tallai snaps his beak. "Do not compare us to the weak-willed human. Our intelligence is far beyond your pitiful imagining."

Salam cackles, and Curran winces at the grinding echo of it in the small space, huffing out another sigh.

"Let's pick this up again tomorrow," he says.

Thank all the holy saints. I feel like I've been awake for a decade.

Curran and I stand, though he manages not to scrape his chair like me. Hunter's wings bracket my torso in their warmth.

"Every second you detain us only worsens your punishment," Tallai says, licking his teeth. "So, go and rest, little humans. Your suffering will come."

Curran mutters something, and yanks open the door. Hunter

herds me from behind. I glimpse Steph straining to see beyond Curran's square head, the flash of a sapphire wing, Greg's ponytail. Steph leans on her bedazzled cane, the day taking its toll.

"And you will suffer most of all, *Maia Buckthorn*," Salam spits.

My name in his beak sends goosebumps shivering up my arms. My knees wobble. I face him with no memory of turning or how I slipped past Hunter's fluffed wings as they arch protectively around me.

Salam stands, his hunched vulture body even more bent with his uninjured wrist cuffed to the table. The metal links strain and screech. The burn on his other wrist looks raw and painful. He sneers at Hunter, then fixes me with his bright eyes.

"Human weakness will deliver your doom. You will witness as I return Hunter to the weapon he is. You will feel his rage, his fists, his teeth. I will reduce you to the whining specimen you were before, but this time you will *perish*."

At first, I think the growl is coming from me because I'm shaking so hard. My teeth are chattering.

But firm and gentle fingers bracelet my biceps and spin me towards the door. Curran scowls—not at me this time—his body still blocking Steph, Greg, and Dev. Steph looks like she's one second from tackling him out the way and battering Salam to death with her cane.

"I am sorry, Maia," Hunter whispers in my ear, his breath chasing the chill from Salam's threat. "I cannot wait any longer."

Then those same firm and gentle fingers guide my stuttering feet through the doorway, and the heavy steel clangs shut behind me.

I gape at my best friends. Haile gapes at all of us, her uniform rumpled from her hours on the hill. She straightens from her slumped position further down the corridor. Curran shoulders me aside and tugs at the door.

"It's jammed," he grunts. "Buckthorn! What the hell is your angel playing at? I let him sit in as a *courtesy*."

A feral grin blooms on Steph's face. "He's giving them what they deserve."

"And what is that?"

"Death," Greg hisses.

Curran stops heaving at the door. I dive for the neighbouring door—thinner steel, with a window—the others cramming in behind me. We pile into the empty viewing room and stare through the one-way glass.

Salam and Tallai are both on their feet, scaly wings flapping as they tug against the cuffs binding them to the table. Hunter stands at the door facing them, a dagger wedged between the frame. A throwing star glows an eerie blue in his hand.

The soulreaver of the flying centipedes. When the heck did he pick that up? I shouldn't be surprised. He attracts bladed weapons like a magnet. I think he might actually *be* a magnet.

Curran punches a button on a speaker panel to the right of the one-way glass. A tiny orange light winks on.

"Hunter!" he barks. "You will desist and remove yourself from that room this instant."

I grab a handful of my commanding officer's khaki uniform and yank him away from the speaker panel. The orange light pings off. I use Curran's momentum to drive him into Dev's arms.

"Hold him for a minute," I say.

Dev wraps his thickly muscled arms around the struggling, pink-cheeked military man. Curran's cap falls off, and the metal badge clinks on the floor. Haile takes a cautious step closer, her hand on the Glock at her hip.

"Haile! Call for backup and detain this brute. Buckthorn has taken leave of her senses. I knew I shouldn't have let a civilian lead an army."

Steph and Greg slot themselves, shoulder to shoulder, in front of Haile.

"Let Maia do what she needs to," Steph says quietly. "And Hunter."

Greg snorts. "Yeah, just try to stop him."

Haile casts me a conflicted glance. Tendrils of hair curl from her bun and stick to her face.

I raise my hands, though Haile hasn't drawn her weapon. Yet.

"I'm going to talk to him. That's all."

Haile's gaze flicks between me and the puffing Curran. Sweat drips onto the slabs of his cheeks. Dev looks bored.

"They're bound and unarmed prisoners, Buckthorn... Maia... You can't..."

"I know. But Hunter can. And will, unless you let me talk to him."

"Brigadier Haile! I order you to get soldiers in here and end this nonsense or I will ensure you are thrown from the military in disgrace."

Dev curls his fingers over Curran's flapping mouth, holding him easily in one arm.

"You talk too much," he says.

"Some things are more important than jobs and glory," I say to Haile.

She closes her eyes, inhales a long breath, then nods. "Do it."

Curran whines a protest into Dev's palm.

Steph smirks and says, "And that's why you were invited to my wedding."

Nothing has changed in the containment room, though I was half-expecting Salam and Tallai to already be dust at Hunter's feet. He can probably hear us through the glass.

I toggle the open channel on the speaker panel, instead of holding down the button, the instructions etched into the metal surroundings.

"I will flay you to the bone for this insult," Salam hisses, his fluorescent gaze narrowed on Hunter, "you ungrateful *wretch*."

"Maia warned you what would happen. As did I."

"You don't have to do this, Hunter," I say, placing my palm on the glass, although he can't see me. "We may let them live, but they'll never be free."

Hunter finds me with his night-penetrating—and apparently mirror-penetrating—midnight-blue eyes. He flips the throwing star across his knuckles, like a magician with a penny.

"Their influence is too great. Too corrupt. They will never rest until they get what they want." Hunter's expression darkens. "They always get what they want. And I love the life that they covet."

"I love you, too, but you don't have to kill them for me."

A smile flickers over Hunter's face. "I do, my tiny wife. For both of us."

Hunter claims a step. Tallai cowers. Fear widens Salam's eyes before he schools his expression to its usual arrogance. He straightens his scrawny neck and flares his dark wings, towering over Hunter despite the short leash of the handcuffs.

"I am your *master*," he hisses through his sharp teeth. "You will drop that weapon and release us."

Hunter dances the throwing star back into his fingers. His next step puts him level with the table.

"Order him to stop, Maia," Haile says, her voice climbing.

158

"I will not listen," Hunter says, not looking at us, though his mouth ticks up. "I have free will. And I made a promise."

"So you would slaughter us while we are chained like dogs?" Salam snarls. "We gave you *life*. Purpose. You exist because of my benevolence."

Hunter side-steps around the table. Salam jerks backwards and slams into Tallai in a leathery flap of wings.

Hunter's smile is as feral as Steph's. "You taught me to kill the weak, did you not? You programmed us to have no compassion."

Hunter lunges and wraps his fingers around Salam's throat. Salam punches at his face, but Hunter's grip only tightens. He lifts the throwing star to Salam's eyeline until his pin-point pupils focus on the glowing blue metal.

"Human! *Maia...*" Salam bleats. "My death will bring retribution you cannot fathom. The guilt for allowing this inhuman act will haunt you to the end of your days. You—"

"Salam'ack'tai'moran," I say, slow and careful, "you brought this on yourself."

Hunter bares his teeth in a predatory grin and draws the point of the throwing star down Salam's cheek. A silvery line of blood wells. Salam chokes.

And crumbles to dust.

Every creature has a soul that can be reaved, even the Creators.

But not the Protectorate.

Hunter wipes his palm on his laced trousers, leaving a pale smear across his thigh. No one breathes in the viewing room. Hunter's boot puffs an imprint into the dust as he moves for Tallai. Tallai dodges his reaching hand.

"Please, no... You cannot! I will give you anything you desire.

Anything!"

Hunter's fist strangles Tallai's begging. He gives no response except for the slow drag of the throwing star down the Creator's cheek.

Tallai should know better than anyone.

Angels are merciless.

23

We hold Uziyah and Abayankari's funeral in The Order of the Holy Angels' church two weeks later. The funerals for the soldiers who lost their lives will go on for months. People pack the pews—Martello Court residents, warrior angels, WAGS. The crowd floods out the door and into the street, where screens have been set up.

Uziyah and Abayankari's portraits flank the coffin on the catafalque—a raised platform—in front of the altar. The oak casket gleams, specially made to fit Uziyah's muscled bulk and broad wings. Abayankari has no coffin, but flowers spill from every surface—white lilies for her and sunflowers for Uziyah. Their photos are the ones from their military identification passes that let them come and go from the barracks, not that anyone could mistake them for anyone else. Or stop them. Uziyah's picture treats his mourners to a haughty smirk. Abayankari looks like she wished grievous bodily harm on the photographer. Or that's her horny face.

It may be morbid, but I plucked a golden feather from Uziyah's wing, and it's mounted in a frame on my living room wall. It's a punch to the heart every time I see it.

I swipe a tear from my cheek. Hunter presses me closer to his side, his arm and wing tucked around me. Steph sits on my left, her hand clasped in mine and resting on my thigh, Greg and Dev beyond her, all of us in the front pew. Bronwyn perches on Hunter's right, her toenails painted black to match her bodysuit. The only colour is the slash of her navy and amethyst eyes and the diamonds of pale blue and pink in her wings. Every part of her droops with sadness.

The whisper of cloth precedes my dad sweeping down the aisle in his purple vestments, the centre embroidered in a band of gold thread. A hush creeps in his wake. He stands behind the lectern and scans the crowd.

He's no longer beholden to the Pope and his orthodoxy, but he loves the trappings of their denomination.

"We have lived through unprecedented times," he says, a hitch in his voice, "yet even this comes as a shock—the first ever funeral for a Holy Angel. It hurts my heart that it is not one, but two for whom we must say our final goodbye."

Quiet sobbing comes from somewhere near the back of the nave. Greg tries to hide a sniffle in his elbow.

"It is especially hard when our last ceremony here was a joyful one to celebrate the union of Stephanie Griffin with her own Holy Angel, Devinon, and her soulmate, Gregory Coltrain."

The trio shuffle beside me and duck their heads.

Dad curls his fingers around the edges of the lectern. "Uziyah approached me afterwards to ask if I would join him and Abayankari in holy matrimony. Of course, I told him he would have to get permission from the good lady herself first."

A ripple of laughter breaks through the pews. I find myself smiling, though my heart is heavy.

"Uziyah and Abayankari had an intense relationship, and it was full of love, which they were not ashamed to share with others."

162

Abayankari definitely propositioned my dad.

"But just because it was unorthodox, does not mean it was wrong." Dad's gaze hesitates on Bronwyn before scooting over the heads of the mourners. "I only wish I could have fulfilled Uziyah's desire to be wed, though I have no doubt their love is eternal and will continue into the afterlife. And that is what we can all hope for—that our love and our memory will go on far longer than our earthly bodies."

Dad pauses to clear his throat and take a sip of water from a pristine glass on the lectern. I run my fingertips through Hunter's velvet feathers, soothed by their softness.

"Now, speaking of unorthodox—today's funeral ceremony will not follow the traditional process. As a humble father and priest, I can only acquiesce to the requests of my daughter, who commands all of us these days."

Steph snorts beside me. I stop stroking Hunter's feathers long enough to pinch the back of her hand.

"With that in mind, I will end my sermon with a quote from Matthew 13:49, after which, Maia will conduct the eulogy for our fallen angels." Dad straightens at the lectern, his eyes softening. "'So it will be at the close of the age. The angels will come out and separate the evil from the righteous.' Amen."

Dad bows and steps to the side, holding his arm out for me to take his place at the lectern. I swallow hard, and Steph gives my hand an encouraging squeeze.

I hate public speaking, but it was either this or listen to my dad drone through bible readings, prayers, and hymns. I had enough of that when I was a kid. And the only god Uziyah and Abayankari believed in was the Creators.

Until recently.

On my five steps to the lectern, I order myself not to open my speech with the word 'okay' or 'right', or risk another smirk-snort from Steph. I pull the cue cards from my black suit pocket and tap them neatly on the lectern. Bodies fidget and cough. I draw a calming breath in and out, then raise my head.

"Uziyah was an arsehole," I say, letting the surprised chuckles swell and fade, "but he was *our* arsehole. And Abayankari... she was a randy psycho who would have destroyed worlds for him. Like my dad said—they were a perfect match."

My throat closes.

Dammit. I knew this would be hard.

I take a sip of my dad's water, and let my eyes drift over the packed pews. Haile tips her head at me, dressed in a navy suit so dark, it may as well be black. She's surrounded by Martello Court residents and angels, isolated from the clump of uniformed WAGS presided by Curran and Reynold.

Curran slapped her with a dishonourable discharge from the army. I thought about banning him from the funeral, but decided I didn't want to be that guy. The ceremony is for everyone to pay their respects to Uziyah and Abayankari, even if they are insufferable douchebags. I'll make it up to Haile somehow.

Curran also informed me that I was no longer welcome in the military, though he thanked me for my efforts.

The pompous prick.

He wanted to throw Hunter in jail for executing Salam and Tallai. He yelled about war crimes and inhumanity. I told him, "Good luck with that." Thankfully, his little bark was drowned by all the others who were glad to hear the Creators got what they deserved.

Including Pat and Dot, and the ten Creators who remained behind on the four surviving spaceships. They were ecstatic, and agreed to cease hostilities if they got to go home. We're negotiating on what will happen to the different Protectorate factions, so they're still taking up a chunk of our sky until then.

I sip another mouthful of water. Shuffle my cue cards.

"I met Uziyah in this church, when he kidnapped me on the command of his masters—may they never rest in peace." That earns me a scowl from Curran, but I don't think I've ever seen him smile, so I ignore it. "Uziyah came from a culture that was brutal beyond imagining, but we gave him choices. We gave him books and naps. A better life. And the last thing he said to me before he died was an expression of gratitude for that freedom. After he told me not to cry."

I'm crying again. Hiccupping. Tears blur the faces watching me. Water drips onto my cue cards and smudges the ink. My voice wobbles, but I force myself to finish.

"I'm glad I got to know Abayankari. The *real* Abayankari. She was terrifying under the influence of the cybernetics, but only mildly alarming as her normal self. Uziyah was the only one sturdy enough to keep up with her." I sniff, and stop myself from wiping my nose on my sleeve. "I'll miss Uziyah calling me feeble creature. He saved my life on the spaceship. He sacrificed himself for me on the battlefield. And I'll never be able to repay that. Abayankari's vengeance saved us all. So remember them, and make sure their deaths were not in vain."

I step from the altar and am engulfed by warmth and ice and the brush of feathers. The church fills with noise while I compose myself.

Then I lead the procession to the crematorium, where we consign Uziyah's body to ash to match his beloved.

24

Hunter keeps his promises. He promised to be gentle. To protect me and be mine, forever and always. He promised Salam and Tallai they would die at his hand for what they did to me.

I took great pleasure in watching their dust be vacuumed from the interview room by the cleaning staff.

And Hunter promised me that when the battle was won, I could do anything I wanted to him.

Anything.

I stand at the foot of our bed and survey my handiwork. Hungry, midnight-blue eyes rake my exposed skin as I tease my nightie over my head and drop it at my feet. Hunter makes a possessive noise low in his throat. My black lace underwear is embroidered with metallic violet and emerald thread to resemble the colour of his wings in a shaft of sunlight.

Beautiful and captivating.

Silken ropes bind my warrior angel to the bed frame at wrist and ankle.

I'll never stop marvelling at his trust in me. His willingness to relinquish control. He's been bound before at the mercy of others, though it was in chains that time and would not have led to anything as pleasant as what I'm about to do to him.

My pulse gushes, swollen at the thought. My pants are already damp, and all I've done is tie him up.

His skin gleams like alabaster, caressed by the flicker of candlelight. The tips of his wings flex in anticipation. Shadows pool beneath sharp cheekbones and gather in the fluttering hollow of his throat. I trail my gaze across broad muscle and the arch of his ribs, no longer marred from the battle and the rip of mutant panther claws.

"Maia," he growls.

The hint of desperation is a starter. A taster. I want him begging.

"Hunter," I say, equally growly. "I'm claiming you as the spoils of war."

A purr rumbles in his chest. "Then claim me."

My knees press into the edge of the mattress. I rub my thumb up the arch of his foot, massaging to his perfect, edible toes. His powerful body melts into the bed. I knead until his eyes are half-lidded and his wings sprawl into puddles of black, then do the same to the other foot. Crawling between his legs, I trail my hands up his calves and massage the pliant muscles of his inner thighs. His hips twitch, dragging his impressive erection across his belly and leaving a slick of pre-cum. I lick him from root to tip and dip my tongue in his slit, savouring his sweet and crisp taste. He chases the heat of my mouth, but I duck my head and suck a testicle instead, tugging and scraping—just a hint—with my teeth.

A groan spills from Hunter, and my name, whispered like a prayer. I resist the urge to rub myself through my soaked panties.

I lave his other ball, petting him with my hands while my mouth is busy—the clefts of muscle at his groin, the ripple of his abdominals, the swell of his pecs. I tweak his nipples and earn a gasp. My tongue traces his firm and flushed crown before I swallow his dick as deep as I can.

Which, let's be honest, is not that deep. The man is *huge*.

Hunter moans and flexes his hips, the head of him easily hitting the back of my throat. But I've had a lot of practise now. I gulp around him, knowing he loves the slick clench of my throat as his dick tries to breach my oesophagus. I hum in encouragement, playing with his balls and the part of his shaft that will never fit in my mouth. I slurp around him and pull off with a satisfying pop.

"Maia... *please*," he pants.

"Soon," I promise.

My lips echo the path of my hands—groin, stomach, chest. I pinch his nipples between my teeth, and his spine bows off the bed. Crouching above him on all fours, I claim his mouth. He kisses me back until we make filthy, wet sounds and I almost forget myself, aching to be filled. Hunter strains to touch more of me. The ropes stretch and creak.

I pull away, breathing heavily, and he tries to chase me. His eyes are all pupil. Drowning black. I stroke his face, and weave my fingers through his hair.

He looks at me as if I'm a goddess. The commander of his heart.

"Show me how good you are with your mouth," I say.

He whines—half-eager, half-pleading. I plant my knees on either side of his head and he arches off the pillow to meet me, the cords in his neck taut. Scorching lips brand between my thighs. My cry echoes off the ceiling. My head falls back, my eyes shut, all my focus on his wicked mouth.

He is ravenous. Moist lips and probing tongue. He purrs

against me when I moan his name and the vibration quivers to my stomach muscles. My thighs tremble as he explores and suckles, drawing more sounds from me. I grip the headboard, bent over him. He meets my eyes as he feasts and fucks me with his tongue.

I climax on a scream and grind against his face. The rush of pleasure sizzles and throbs. The greedy suck of his mouth extends the orgasm and pushes me to the brink of madness. I sit hard on his chest, floppy and sated, and he smirks at me. I lick the taste of myself from his shiny lips. His ribs heave beneath my bare arse.

I scramble backwards, always the frantic one. I wrap a hand around his erection, unable to close my fist completely, but pause with his crown cradled by the folds of my opening. Hunter holds himself still, though his eyes are wild and his pulse throbs at his throat. A delicate shiver passes from him to me.

"I love you, Maia," he says, his voice husky.

I smile. "I love you, too."

He breaches me, guided by my hand. I sink lower, achingly slow, drawing a noise from Hunter that's both pained and pleased. My savage angel tugs on his arm and the rope snaps. Scalding fingers brand my hip and seat me until I'm stretched and full and where I'm meant to be. His grunt of relief starts a burn of pleasure in the pit of my gut, flaming to where he impales me. I rise on wobbling knees, dragging and squeezing my inner walls along his length before I sink all the way back down, punching a guttural sound from my lungs. His fingers tighten, coaxing me to meet his thrusts as I glide in and out. My skin swells, already so close. Hunter looks wrecked. Pushed to his limit from the rock of my hips.

My pulse thunders in my ears, my throat, my groin. Hunter sighs my name each time he buries himself inside me.

And just as I'm reaching the crest, as Hunter's frenzied pace matches mine, my phone peals.

I yelp, nearly toppling from Hunter.

"I should've turned that goddamn thing off," I grumble.

I circle my hips.

"Are you going to answer it?" Hunter says through his teeth, his hair flopping into his eyes and sticking to his cheekbones.

"I'll call her back. I couldn't stop right now even if you begged me."

"I would not beg you to stop. Never you."

With a ping of tortured cloth, Hunter releases his other arm. Both hands clamp my waist and drive me onto him. Our cries smother the ringing phone. He rails me into a muscle-clenching, spine-tingling orgasm that leaves me shrieking and boneless, though I have enough senses left to feel him come, the spurt of him so hard inside me, it scatters the rest of my wits.

I slump on top of my panting warrior angel. Our heartbeats drum together, but eventually settle. A warm palm cups my butt and holds me in place. Speared and happy. A sleepy hush settles over the room.

My phone trills again.

I huff into Hunter's chest, slapping at the bedside cabinet without lifting my head.

"What's up, Bronwyn?" I croak.

"Child... hurry. You must come here. Please—come."

I jerk upright, biting my lip on a moan as Hunter shifts inside me, no less rigid than when we started. He could easily go another round. Definitely two. Maybe three, until my body

170

weeps for mercy.

My tortured heart kicks, confused between panic and the promise of fun. "What's wrong?"

"They have called. You must come, child. Come *now*."

The line goes dead.

25

I stand on the crags of Arthur's Seat and stare at the unending blackness of the spaceship swallowed by the night. Lights streak the uneven surface. An airlock gapes open in front of us—the very one we stumbled from when I parked the stolen vessel on home soil. I stare into the darkness, hesitating. My husband and best friends are silent yet supportive at my back, though we've been here for ten minutes and I haven't moved.

After yanking our clothes on—hoodie, jeans, and trainers for me, black laced top, trousers, and boots for Hunter—I phoned Bronwyn back. She babbled no new information in her state of agitation, only that we needed to get to the ship. Urgently.

Of course it has to do with the Creators. Has another province threatened us? Are the four Protectorate ships that remained behind barrelling through space to teach us the error of our ways? Maybe they learned of Salam and Tallai's demise and it spurred them to come and make us regret.

Of course it's not over. Of *course* we can't be left to live in peace. Our victory was nothing but a tiny reprieve before the next battle, like it's been since the angel apocalypse.

I can't face another war. More death. Our fight was short and intense, but I'd hoped it would be the last. I always hope it will be the last.

I glance at the dark, velvet sky. Blobs and lines of white mark the positions of the four empty ships. Pat, Dot, and the other Creators are currently enjoying human hospitality and are curiously witnessing what happens when we destroy the cybernetics of their Protectorate. A process that will continue for many months to remove them all and observe the results.

I suck in a breath, hold it, and sigh it back out. "Okay, let's go."

Several hands squeeze and pat my back. Greg has the grace not to grumble, but then it is a mild summer's night. Dev's sapphire wings bracket his husband and wife.

"You're a queen of warriors," Steph says, leaning on her bedazzled cane. "You've fucking got this."

Greg has a final puff on his vape. "Yeah, what she said."

Steam trails from his lips. The sharp yet comforting scent of weed winds around our small group. I square my shoulders and step up into the spaceship. Light blooms in the receiving chamber, though there's no obvious source. I hustle through the open double doors into a corridor of pearly walls and turquoise floor.

I expect fear or nausea, maybe a panic attack as I'm assaulted by memory, but I feel nothing except melancholy at the reminder of the colour of Abayankari's eyes.

Therapy works, who knew. Or perhaps all I needed was the deaths of my tormentors to remove the stain they left on my soul.

My trainers squeak on the polished floor. I need some prompting to navigate the spirals and forks since I've not stepped on the ship for almost two years, excluding my brief healing visit after the battle where I was too woozy to feel much of anything. Bronwyn meets us in a flap of scaly wings before we reach the domed room of screens—the heart of the vessel.

She wrings her hands in front of her hunched chest, clicking her beak in distress. "Thank goodness you are finally here, child. Come. Quickly now."

She bobs away on her stork legs and I hustle to keep up, everyone slotting in behind me.

"Is my dad here?"

Bronwyn doesn't turn around. "He retired to my room to offer us privacy."

Our rapid footsteps and the thud of Steph's cane echo in the corridors. Everything looks the same. Bronwyn whirls at the archway into the control room, and I jerk back into Hunter's chest to avoid a slap from her wing. Hunter's hands wrap around my biceps to steady me.

"You must... *please* be deferential. You must. Come."

Bronwyn spins, and stalks into the grey control room. I share a glance with Steph, my eyebrows raised. Bronwyn's spread wings block the bank of screens. The silver dome of the ceiling reflects her figure and my group of five. She throws herself flat, beak and bones clacking on the ground. The floor slopes to the raised dais. At first, I think all the screens are black until something moves in the central monitor. My gasp slips out.

"Woah," Greg says.

We stutter into a line behind the prostrated Bronwyn. Dev and Hunter share a look, then drop smoothly to one knee, their heads bowed and their wings rustling on the floor.

"Bloody hell," I whisper, inching closer to Steph and Greg.

"I have summoned Maia as you requested, my lords," Bronwyn chitters in a high voice from her sprawled position. "She is accompanied by her trusted advisers, the humans, Steph and

Greg, and the angels—the quooritai—Hunter and Devinon."

Quooritai? Is that the name of the angels' species? Why have I never heard it before?

On the central screen, two shapes stand wing to wing and form a living shadow. Two shirivaks. There's not a hint of colour in their black skin and wings. Even their beaks are black. Their eyes are a slash of fluorescent violet that leaves afterimages when I blink. Bony crests stretch as tall as sails.

"We are grateful for your swiftness, Bronwyn'challi," the Creator on the right says. His voice is no mere buzz or click, like Salam or Tallai, but the ancient grind of stone. The shift of tectonic plates over aeons.

"You may rise, Bronwyn'challi." The Creator on the left dips their head, her voice no less grinding or prehistoric. "As may you, our warriors."

Creators who express thanks and don't demand constant worship. This is... new.

Bronwyn leaps upright in an ungainly scuffle of wings and elbows. Hunter and Dev straighten elegantly—because of course they do. Steph and Greg nudge me a step forward, the traitors. Two pairs of bright eyes fasten on me. I wave, and immediately feel stupid.

"We are grateful for your attendance at this impromptu audience, Maia," the first Creator says.

"What"—a quick peek at Bronwyn—"can I call you?"

Two beaks open to bare rows of teeth.

"Bronwyn'challi has described your difficulty with the pronunciation of our names," the second Creator says. "We find that... humbling. You may call me Nishay. My esteemed colleague is Jamaiio."

I join them in the head bobbing. "It's... interesting to meet you."

That's as polite as I can be until I know what they want.

"We are the shirivak contingent of the Creator Assembly," Jamaiio says, as if reading my mind. "Together with our elected counterparts, we rule the sectors."

The Creators lean back, revealing the room behind them—grey walls, silver dome, sloping floor.

Bronwyn said they could communicate ship to ship across universes.

Unless they're already in ours.

"Sectors?" I say.

Jamaiio cocks his bird head. "We are the peak of our empire. Below the Assembly are the sectors, regions, provinces, then Protectorate factions. We rule them all."

Did Salam and Tallai inflate their own importance? The way they spoke was as if they were a step down from absolute leadership, but there are more levels to the hierarchy than I thought.

"Tell me, Maia, what happened to the generals of the Romshalla Province—Salam'ack'tai'moran and Tallai'sig'chai?" Nishay says, her gaze unwavering and intent.

I suppress a shiver.

Should I lie? No. We haven't done anything wrong except survive and defend ourselves.

I lift my chin. "Salam and Tallai received the punishment they deserved, and are no longer breathing."

The Creators snap their beaks. Scaly wings slither together. Steph and Greg wince.

"We have heard much on their actions of late," Jamaiio says. "Pray tell us, in your own words, why they deserved such a fate."

Thank goodness I didn't lie.

"When they sent their angels... the quooritai... to teach us a lesson, we fought back and won fairly. A portion of the warriors chose to stay and we welcomed them, since our civilisation believes in free will." I try not to let judgement seep into my voice, and fail. "We learned from their attack and implemented ways to be greener to protect our environment. We replicated some of your clean technology to help us. But Salam and Tallai were too proud to accept their defeat."

"Arseholes," Steph hisses, earning a sharp look from Bronwyn.

Steph schools her face into an expression of innocence. A chortle rumbles in Bronwyn's throat, but doesn't escape her beak.

"The quooritai kidnapped me, Steph, Greg, and our angels who chose a peaceful life on Earth and took us into your universe on their spaceship, where they wanted to make an example of us. They collared our angels to enhance their cybernetics." I swallow hard, my chest aching. Hunter sways towards me, but I shake my head. "We loved our angels. They became part of our civilisation and we saw what they could be when they were happy. Hunter is... Hunter is my soulmate. My forever. The same goes for Dev with Steph and Greg. Salam and Tallai used that bond against us. They got Hunter to hurt me, again and again, hoping I would break."

I swipe at a tear. Bronwyn's pretty eyes soften in sympathy, and she tilts her head towards me. Nishay and Jamaiio observe in silence.

"Did you know Salam and Tallai raped their warriors?" I say, my voice hot. "And encouraged them to rape each other in brutal dominance fights?"

Nishay and Jamaiio turn to share a glance, their long beaks and bony crests in profile.

"We did not know this," Nishay says solemnly. "Please continue."

"Salam and Tallai's plan to break me almost succeeded. But I had allies—Uziyah of the quooritai, and Bronwyn." I return Bronwyn's bow. "We freed Steph and Greg, and commandeered the ship. I told Salam and Tallai to leave us alone, then fired them into the Oort Cloud in an escape pod. I could have killed them, as they were so eager to do to me. They abused that mercy and attacked Earth with six Protectorate factions. We taught *them* a lesson this time."

"What of the captured Protectorate?" Jamaiio says, peering closer through the screen. "That is an immense force to bend to your will. A force that can control star systems."

"Their cybernetics are being removed so they can make their own choices beyond violence and subservience." I smile at Hunter. At each of my friends. "I adopted the angels and they *chose* to fight for me to defend our planet from tyranny. The rest of the Protectorate will be given the same choice." I glare at the ancient Creators. "Unless we can finally live in peace and I have no need of an army."

Bronwyn fidgets and flutters her wings. Hunter and Dev treat the Creators to the stern stare of a warrior angel.

"You would return the Protectorate into our care?" Jamaiio says slowly.

"I would give them the choice. We'll welcome any who want to stay and not hinder any who want to leave. But I'd expect them to be allowed to live how they please, no matter where they end up."

The Creators' silent eyeball communication lasts a long time.

Steph and Greg shuffle behind me.

"We rule countless sectors," Nishay says after a pause, each word chosen carefully. "The sectors manage the regions. The provinces are minuscule fractions of our fleet, but are trusted to be autonomous, though we supervise and guide, when requested. It seems Salam'ack'tai'moran and Tallai'sig'chai took that autonomy and were... harsher than we taught them to be. The cybernetics are for communication and the enhancement of natural abilities, not hyper-aggression. As a last resort, they are used for control, since our Protectorate are far stronger than their Creators. But strength is needed to protect all life. Strength and, sometimes, punishment."

Jamaiio bares his teeth in a smile. "However, I believe this is an opportunity for experimentation. And we do love to experiment."

Nishay chuckles. "Indeed. Perhaps a milder hand will tame our wayward civilisations, with stricter methods should that fail."

"Agreed," Jamaiio says, clacking his beak.

The two Creators return their attention to our somewhat confused group.

"We look forward to seeing your results," Nishay says.

I meet the blinding eyes of each Creator. "What—and I say this with all due respect—the hell are you talking about?"

"Maia Buckthorn of the planet Earth," Jamaiio and Nishay say in perfect synchrony, "will you accept the mantle of responsibility and lead your province with the respect and merciful hand it deserves?"

"*My* province?!" I squeak, while Steph hoots gleefully behind me.

26

18 Months Later

"Maia, come look at this!" Greg shouts, darting through the archway into the control room. "It's so awesome, man."

I roll my eyes at him, but turn my fond smile to Haile. "You all right at the helm while I go see whatever rock or cloud or star he's excited about today?"

"Sure thing, Boss," she says with a smirk. "Bronwyn will keep me right."

Another eye roll.

Honestly, as soon as I invited Haile to join us on our interplanetary mission, Steph wasted no time in convincing her to be a co-conspirator—excuse me, glamorous assistant. The two of them have been inseparable, despite the age difference.

Curran wanted to come. He was quite adamant about getting a seat on the ship and graciously promised to follow my command. I told him his offer was appreciated, but his services were not required.

"Do not fret, child," Bronwyn says, peering over Haile's shoulder at the central screen of the control console. "Unlike our previous journey, I now know what I am looking at."

Nishay and Jamaiio talked us through the steps of how to pilot the spaceship, including the procedure for taking off from Arthur's Seat. We left the old volcano a lot flatter than it used to be.

Thirteen months have passed since then, though we've only been awake for one of them. We stayed in goo-sleep until the Oort Cloud, then travelled through the wormhole to the Creators' star system. The sight of the green and gold planet with its five small moons gave me a shiver—Salam and Tallai's home.

Thankfully, it's not our destination. On the enthusiastic invite of Nishay and Jamaiio, we're heading to their planet on the other side of the blue-white sun. They want to hold a ceremony in our honour and train us—or me—how to properly lead the Protectorate and rule a province.

Hunter joins me at my side and takes my hand as we follow Greg's bouncing gait out the archway and into the shining corridor of pearl and turquoise.

Hunter smirks. "He really is like a puppy."

"I heard that," Greg sings without turning around.

"You were meant to."

Greg skips off down the corridor, dodging warrior angels as they walk and swoop. They greet me as I pass.

Ten of our Jewels, Markian included, chose to stay on Earth. The goodbyes were hard, though I'll see them again, even if it's decades from now.

As part of our welcoming ceremony, Nishay and Jamaiio will be sharing more Creator technology. An injection that'll grant me and my human advisers a life as extended as a warrior angel's, or any of the Protectorate and Creators. It's not immortality, but it's a bloody long time.

I slide a peek at Hunter striding beside me. Black hair falls into dark eyes. His clothes hug his broad shoulders, narrow hips, and long legs. His wing brushes my back, curling protectively against the bustle of the corridor despite his hand in mine.

"I still can't believe you're two hundred and thirty-two years old," I say.

He grins at me. "I may be two centuries your senior, but I still have the stamina of youth."

"Oh, I know you have the stamina."

The grin morphs into a smirk.

My muscles have been aching for days. Hunter promised to replace my bad memories of the ship with good ones. Sexy ones. It involves christening quite a lot of rooms.

"Hurry up, you two," Greg calls ahead, before disappearing down a fork in the corridor.

Hunter snorts, cocking his head. "Your pets have escaped their leash again."

I hear the skitter of claws two seconds later. Excited yips ripple down the passage. I spin and drop to my knees, my arms open. Two foforolona barrel into me in a streak of black, and butt my chin. They weave around me, their spiked tails whipping. Purrs rumble in their broad chests.

"Sorry, Maia," my dad says, puffing to catch up. "They slipped past me without even trying. Bad kitties."

"Yes, very bad kitties," I coo, rubbing their foreheads around their eye stalks. The purring gets louder.

Their soulreaving body parts stopped working as soon as their cybernetics were removed. The scientists at Roslin tried different ways to communicate with them, but their intelligence seems to be on par with a dog or a cat. They milled around in their cage looking lost. I forced myself to visit, despite one of their kind having killed Uziyah, and two of them galloped over to the viewing window, shrieking and rubbing against it until I went inside and gave them some attention. They've been my shadows ever since.

They don't have names they respond to beyond their sequence of creation. I call them Five and Seven, because five thousand and two, and seven thousand three hundred and ninety-eight is a bit of a mouthful. They love to curl into shiny doughnuts and nap on any soft surface.

The scientists called it imprinting. Several more latched on to members of the public and WAGS when we opened the viewings to a wider audience. Those who didn't choose an 'owner', so to speak, are returning with us on our ship.

The warrior angels like to play with them. It's adorable.

I straighten and click my fingers. "Come on then, you two. But you'd better behave."

They look up at me with identical expressions of devotion. Five's eyes are a soft lavender, but Seven has three different colours—orange, red, and yellow. They treat Hunter to a leg rub, then pad along behind us, flanking my dad.

"So where are we going?" Dad says.

"Greg has something to show us."

Dad sighs. "It's not another constellation, is it?"

We take the fork in the corridor and find Greg dancing with impatience. He brightens, scuttling ahead. Above him, a small group of Protectorate whirr by on dragonfly wings.

I wasn't surprised to find survivors in the crashed spaceship that fell with a full contingent of warriors. The Protectorate are a hardy bunch. They have insectile heads and a humanoid body, plus the translucent wings.

We returned to the Creators' universe in a convoy of five—our ship, Pat and Dot with their slime puddles, and the three vessels transporting the grey aliens, green Minotaurs, and flying centipedes. Those who chose not to remain on Earth, anyway. As soon as the wormhole spat us out, we were met by the four ships that disobeyed Salam and Tallai and remained behind to tattle to the Assembly.

I'm sure we're causing quite a stir as we cross the solar system together.

Greg beckons to us, then disappears through an archway. The room opens into a huge observation deck that ends in a massive window onto the stars and the black eternity of space. Steph and Dev wave at us before returning their attention to the view. We join them at the window.

"Look," Greg breathes, fogging the not-glass.

A coppery planet sits amongst the blackness, orbited by two golden moons. Silvery clouds swirl across its surface.

Nishay and Jamaiio's home planet. Are they watching us approach?

Greg presses his nose to the window. "And when Alexander saw the breadth of his domain he wept, for there were no more worlds to conquer."

"Are you quoting something, prickles?" Steph says, her eyebrow arched. "Feels like you're quoting something."

"Who's Alexander?" I say, my gaze on the new, and hopefully welcoming, planet.

"You guys are so uneducated," Greg scoffs. "It's a famous quote about Alexander the Great. He was a military philosopher and warrior. It's supposedly something Plutarch said—describing Alexander when he'd conquered all the nations he wanted to conquer." Greg's eyes sparkle. "According to Hans

Gruber in *Die Hard*, anyway."

"Not exactly apt for our situation, prickles. We were invited."

"Maybe not now, but for when we get sent out to the misbehaving civilisations. Ones we've not conquered yet." Greg huffs. "Okay, you ruined it."

"Well, as general of this province, I'm not going to follow in the great Alexander's footsteps."

Steph smirks and says, "Maia the Great."

"We're not here to conquer," I say as the Creators' planet draws closer and our future unravels into the unknown. "We're here to save them—even if it's from themselves."

The End

Let Me Know What You Think!

What did you think of the finale? Do you hate me for killing off Uziyah and Abayankari? It hurt to do it, I swear. Leave me a review and let me know. I enjoy hearing from my readers. Reviews also help me find other people, like you, who'll love my books.

Can't wait to hear from you!

For a bonus epilogue of Maia and Hunter out in the world turning mundane activities to badass adventures, join my mailing list at nadinelittle.com/bonus-epilogue by scanning the QR code below:

Want more apocalyptic brutality with a dose of romance (once you get past the torture)?
Try *Captivity*, book 1 in *The Faction War Chronicles*

Join Anita Carmichael in a bloody Scotland on her quest to find out who murdered her sister and started a war.

About the Author

Nadine Little lives in Scotland and is an ecologist who loves botany. This may be one of her few series without anything resembling a dragon. The story came about when she'd reached a snag in her novel *Verdana* and had no idea how it was going to end. As a break, she decided to write about the soothing topics of global catastrophe and surviving an angel apocalypse.

You're welcome.

For more on her books and a peek behind the scenes, sign up to her mailing list and follow her on social media.

You can connect with me on:
- https://nadinelittle.com/https://nadinelittle.com
- https://twitter.com/Nadine_Little_
- https://www.facebook.com/nadinelittleauthor

Subscribe to my newsletter:
- https://nadinelittle.com/bonus-epilogue